The Year
the
Swallow
Came E

The Year the Swallows Came Early

KATHRYN FITZMAURICE

THE BOWEN PRESS
An Imprint of HarperCollins*Publishers*

Library of Congress Cataloging-in-Publication Data
Fitzmaurice, Kathryn.
   The year the swallows came early / by Kathryn Fitzmaurice. —
1st ed.
      p.   cm.
   Summary: After her father is sent to jail, eleven-year-old
Groovy Robinson must decide if she can forgive the failings of
someone she loves.
   ISBN 978-0-06-162497-1 (trade bdg.)
   ISBN 978-0-06-162499-5 (lib. bdg.)
   [1. Fathers and daughters—Fiction.   2. Forgiveness—
Fiction.   3. Prisoners—Fiction.   4. Conduct of life—Fiction.]
I. Title.
PZ7.F5776Ye   2009   2008020156
[Fic]—dc22   CIP
                                                       AC

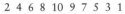
2 4 6 8 10 9 7 5 3 1
❖
First Edition

For Sam,
world's best electric guitar player,

and for Hugh,
who made us get a dog.
(We don't know what took us so long!)

CONTENTS

Coconut Flakes · 1

The Louisiana in Mama · 14

Five-Star Chocolate-Covered Strawberries · 22

Tortillas in Cellophane Wrap · 31

Orange-Flavored Tums · 38

Blue Flip-Flops Really Worn Down · 47

What Frankie Did when He Took the Dinghy Out · 56

Fish Sticks · 65

Our Usual Table by the Fire Pit · 71

Flashlights and Chocolate Bars · 79

Two Specials to Go · 86

In Front of the Mermaid · 91

Jasmine Tea with Limes · 100

Saltines and Liquid Tylenol · 105

Coffee *con Leche* · 109

Chocolate Ice Cream versus Vanilla Ice Cream · 116

Frankie's Favorite Kind of Sandwich · 121

The Part of Marisol that Shines · 127

The (Big) Cardboard Box in the Hall Closet · 135

Burned Tuna Melts · 143

Fancy Signature with Loops on the *E* and the *R* · 154

Nothing · 166

El Niño · 169

Not Sloppy Joes with Sweet Onions · 171

How to Make a List · 179

Cinnamon Churro but No Root Beer · 184

Vacation Memory · 193

Strawberries Gone Bad · 198

The Scout · 200

White Chocolate · 206

Petrochelidon Pyrrhonota · 213

A Pillowcase Full of
Halloween Candy · 219

Card Game · 224

A Nice Tuna Fish Casserole with Peas · 230

Forks + Knives = Monopoly Dice · 239

Spaghetti out of a Jar · 246

Scrambled Eggs · 251

Cleanup on Aisle Two · 257

Caramel · 262

The Year
the
Swallows
Came Early

COCONUT FLAKES

We lived in a perfect stucco house, just off the sparkly Pacific, with a lime tree in the backyard and pink and yellow roses gone wild around a picket fence. But that wasn't enough to keep my daddy from going to jail the year I turned eleven. I told my best friend, Frankie, that it was hard to tell what something was like on the inside just by looking at the outside. And that our house was like one of those See's candies with beautiful swirled chocolate on the outside, but sometimes hiding coconut flakes on the inside, all gritty and hard, like undercooked white rice.

Things that look just right come undone quicker than the last day of summer. And one day, it happened right in front of me. The horoscope Mama read to me that morning should've been enough warning: *Expect the unexpected.* I'd raised my eyebrows and smiled, thinking the unexpected might be finally discovering a way to chop onions without crying or finding a dollar on the street— something unexpected but in a good way.

It wasn't.

Officer Miguel surprised Daddy and me, stopping us as we were walking out of the Swallow Shop & Ferry on our way into town. I walked with Daddy on his way to work every Saturday because I had no school bus to catch then.

"Mitch?" the officer asked my daddy. "There's a problem." He stood on the main corner of town, like he'd been waiting for us. Like he knew we'd be there at this time on this day.

"What problem?" I asked. I looked up at Daddy, thinking he must've forgotten to pay another parking ticket.

"I can't be late for work. I just started a new job at the hardware store," Daddy told the officer. "I'm sure this can wait." He took my hand quickly like he suddenly remembered he needed to get to an appointment, and we started across the street.

"But—" I turned to look back at Officer Miguel.

"Let's go," Daddy told me, pulling my arm just a little.

"You better take a look at this." Officer Miguel ran up to us fast, waving some papers, leaving his patrol car parked on the street.

Daddy sighed and stopped on the opposite sidewalk, where someone had used gray chalk to draw a small bird flying over a tree. His left foot covered the leaves of the tree and half the bird. He squeezed my hand hard, like he was trying to decide what to do. But then he let go softly, and his hand fell to his side.

"What's going on?" I asked him.

But he didn't answer. Instead, he watched the

sky for what seemed like a million minutes—and just then, it seemed perfectly stitched to the horizon in the west where the cumulus clouds made shapes—like he was looking for an answer. Like he was waiting for the clouds to form the words, *Say this*. . . . Finally he pointed to the side of the road without looking at me or telling me anything.

So I walked there, knowing he wanted me to by the way he pushed his lips together. He held his arm high and stiff, like a command to go to my room.

Maybe it's true there's no such thing as a sign from above, but as I stepped onto that curb, I felt something. Even worse, I noticed Mr. Tom, the homeless man, suddenly standing up the street looking like he knew something too. Like he was saying, *Groovy Robinson, be ready, because things could be changing.*

My hands became sweaty. I waited while Officer Miguel showed Daddy the papers, trying to steer clear of Mr. Tom. I crossed and uncrossed my arms a million times. They had a mind of their own. Finally I pushed my hands deep into the pockets of my jean skirt just to keep them still.

I'm here to tell you I listened the best I could, but every time Officer Miguel talked, it was too hushed.

Daddy was louder and angrier than I'd ever heard him. And he kept taking little steps backward. And I kept thinking that he should not be talking to that policeman like he was.

Then I saw his shoulders slump down. He got into the backseat of the police car while Officer Miguel stuffed his handcuffs back into his pocket, like he'd decided it wasn't going to be necessary to use force.

Mr. Tom covered his face with his hands and sat down on the curb.

I ran over to the car as fast as I could, blinking tears back into my eyes. I wondered what Daddy could've done to make Officer Miguel put him in his car. I told myself, *Don't cry, don't you even think about crying. Who cares if they have to take him away? He'll be back after everything gets straightened out.*

"I can't go into this right now, Groovy," Daddy told me through the crack in the window. His eyes shrank to the size of tiny dots, and his face turned stiff. Quiet floated between us, the kind that makes people uncomfortable when there's nothing to say.

Then he seemed to change his mind about talking, and with a sad voice he said, "Sometimes when you figure out the answer to a problem—something you *know* you need to fix—it's too late. You know what you have to do, but you've run out of time." His eyes looked at me, but like I wasn't there. "Groovy, listen to me." He put his hand on the window, his fingers smudging the glass. "Things can start out on track, but end up different. I'm sorry." And he looked away before I could say anything.

"Groovy, is your mother at work today?" Officer Miguel asked me.

"Yes, sir," I answered, but it didn't sound like the normal me.

"So she knows where you are then?" He

looked me over good, like he was trying to decide if he should call my mama. But everyone knew I mostly took care of myself on weekends. And Mama worked right up the street anyway, not more than fifty steps north.

"Yes, she knows where I am," I said, like half of me was saying the words and the other half was thinking, *Excuse me, Officer Miguel, but you must have the wrong man.*

Frankie came running out from the Swallow, where he'd been helping out his stepbrother, Luis. "Is everything okay?"

"He's taking my daddy," I told him.

The police radio in the car called out instructions. I could hear it saying Daddy's name with a blurring sound of numbers that sounded like some sort of code.

"Groovy, I'm going to have to leave with your father now," Officer Miguel told me. He looked sad as he wrote in a small notebook and then flipped it closed. Being one of two policemen who lived in our town, he knew everybody's business.

"I'm sorry, honey," he said. "You should go see your mother. Tell her I have your father."

I nodded that I understood.

Frankie grabbed my hand and held on tight. Looking back now, I know he did this to keep me from falling down. Frankie's like that.

"Maybe we should sit over here," he said, walking me to the yellow wooden bench right outside the Swallow's front door as we watched the police car drive off. It turned the corner with only the back of my daddy's head showing through the rear window.

"Do you know why the police are taking him away?" Frankie asked finally, trying not to talk too loud, trying to be sweet to me.

"No," I answered. I had no idea. It was true Daddy seemed to get the kind of bosses who ended up firing him. And that just last month his job selling houses had gone bad. But people hardly ever went to jail for getting fired, and he always found a new job sooner or later.

Mama didn't like him always changing jobs.

Sometimes she said things about him that I wouldn't repeat to anyone. Like we were better off with him not around all the time. And that closet skeletons and trouble summed Daddy up.

I thought we all lived in a straightforward Betty Crocker kind of way. But she thought it might be a good idea for Daddy to try living in an apartment for a while. That in the long run, a Cancer—her—and a Sagittarius—him—couldn't stay together.

I didn't pay attention to her when she talked like that. I'd say, "I'm not listening, I can't hear you," with my hands pressed over my ears to keep the sound out. I knew she didn't always see things the way Daddy did.

They couldn't even agree on my name.

It was Daddy who'd started calling me Groovy, instead of my given name, Eleanor Robinson. Mama had given me the name Eleanor Robinson after her grandmother, on account of her being a famous writer of science fiction novels. Mama said it would be good luck for me because luck skipped to every fourth generation in our family.

Then one day when I was two years old, Daddy took me to work with him because Mama's hair salon didn't allow toddlers running about. While he was fixing cars at the gas station, which was his career before selling houses, he used to play the radio real loud. He said I danced all day, stopping only at lunchtime to eat oyster crackers. From then on he called me Groovy. Even now, Mama only calls me Eleanor when she's trying to impress someone. Like a teacher.

Daddy always did things like that. Things like changing my name without Mama's permission. And now I was going to have to tell Mama that the police had taken him away. Something else she wouldn't like.

"I've never known anyone who's gone to jail before." I could barely say it. But I figured that's where they were taking him.

"Me neither," Frankie answered.

The morning heat curled around us. I felt my

T-shirt sticking to my skin and the air pressing down hard.

Mama called this earthquake weather, and she went around flushing all the toilets in our house to make sure there was fresh water in the tank in case we needed it in an emergency. Because according to her, when the temperature rose above eighty degrees and it wasn't even summer yet, the ground got restless.

"About that, Mama," I said to her every time she brought it up. "Miss Johnson told us that there's no such thing as earthquake weather, that earthquakes just happen on their own." But Mama would always roll her eyes and tell me my teacher hadn't had enough life experiences to understand the forces of nature.

Mama was so afraid of earthquakes, and that one would come before she'd had the chance to wash her hair and apply her makeup for the day, that she kept a box filled with pink foam curlers and free samples of cosmetics and hair products under the kitchen sink. All this so we would be ready for the Big One when it came and the whole state of California separated from the rest of the U.S., floating off on its own.

I didn't worry much about those quakes the way she did, being born in California and used to them since I was a baby. I'd tell her, "A little shaking; no big deal."

Unlike Mama, who at sixteen moved here from Louisiana, where all the ground does is slowly sink deeper below sea level every year. They couldn't even bury people after they died in Louisiana where she came from because sooner or later, they'd float back up to the surface. Instead they built little houses for them and kept them on top of the ground, safe and sound.

"Do you want something to drink?" Frankie asked in his helpful voice, because it was so hot. He knew what people needed before they did. For a person in sixth grade, he was pretty smart. Once a customer came into the Swallow and Frankie said, and I quote, "You look like you could use an Orangina and one of Luis's tacos." That customer looked at Frankie, amazed because what Frankie said was exactly what he wanted, right then and there.

"Yeah, but no thanks," I said, getting up. "I have to go."

"If you're gonna tell your mom, I can come with you." He stood up straight and stiff, like he was comparing himself to someone else to see who was taller.

"It's okay," I told him. "I should tell her by myself."

And I started running as fast as I could up the hill, thinking that this had to be some kind of mistake. And Mama and I would straighten it out right away.

THE LOUISIANA IN MAMA

"Mama!" I stood outside the open door of the hair salon where Mama worked and waved to get her attention.

She turned quickly and held up her finger. I knew she liked to give her clients all of her attention while they sat in her chair. But with Daddy being taken away, I was going to have to talk to her right in the middle of an appointment.

I ran to the open windows where she stood in front of her station so she could see I was there about something real important this time. The smell of hair dye, melons, and damp towels drifted out.

"I *need* to talk to you," I whispered loudly to her.

"I'm almost done, Groovy."

"But it's really *important*."

"You'll have to wait a minute. Please don't be so impulsive. You know you do that." She said it politely, but looked at me a second longer than normal, like an exclamation mark in code. Because according to her, with me being a Leo, I had tendencies toward impulsiveness.

"You sure are a genius, Lilliana!" said the lady sitting in Mama's chair. She stared at herself in the big mirror. "I think dyeing my hair blond looks really good. Can I wash it tomorrow, or should it rest another day?"

Mama unsnapped the black cape around the lady's neck and swung the chair around to look her in the face. "You can wash it tomorrow, honey," she told her. "I only use professional products that hold up to the elements."

If there was one thing Mama knew about, it was bleach. Her own hair was bleached, but she always denied it, saying she was a natural blond like I was. Mama said she had to keep herself looking good. After all, she was in the business of looking good.

She was sort of famous around town. Once she even did an old-time movie star's hair. The story goes that while the movie star was on vacation, she had some kind of hair emergency, and her usual hairdresser couldn't be reached on such short notice. Well, because the Secret Styling Hair and Nail Salon is listed in the phone book as taking walk-ins, she'd rushed right over wearing a hat and sunglasses so no one would recognize her. Mama had a picture of herself standing next to the woman framed in gold, hanging on the wall by her mirror. She said she'd been expecting that great things would happen to her that day because her horoscope had predicted it.

Mama's client admired herself once more and then stood up to say good-bye.

I ran back to the front door and made my way inside. I knew this was the kind of thing Mama would say was nobody's business but ours.

"Thank you, Lilliana," the client told my mama. "By the way, where did you get that extraordinary wood carving of the mermaid by your mirror? Is it for sale?"

"No," I told her as I stomped toward Mama. "It's not."

Mama glared at me like I'd thrown a water balloon at her, soaking her hair and clothes. "I'll be right with you," she told me. Then she smiled real big at her client, as though I hadn't interrupted.

"Oh, no," she told her. "This used to be a piece of driftwood that came from the waters of Mexico, where the humpback whales mate every January. For hundreds of years those whales have been going back every winter to that same protected bay. And they always know the way. I don't suppose they have maps on the bottom of the ocean."

"Excuse me," I said, as polite as possible, aiming my words at her client. "I'm *very* sorry to keep interrupting, but I really need to talk to my mama."

"Of course, dear." She smiled nice and packed up her purse to leave, her new blond hair shining as she walked out the door.

Mama gave me a look that said, *Haven't I taught you any manners?* Then she arranged the mermaid on her table next to a purple quartzite rock.

As long as I'd been coming to see her at work, these two things were always around her station. She was more apt to believe in superstition and her signs rather than Jesus Christ, our Lord and Savior. She said it was the Louisiana in her.

"All right, Groovy." She unplugged her blow-dryer and quickly swept up the stray pieces of hair around her chair. "What is so important?"

"I think we should talk outside," I told her, feeling tears start in my eyes again. And for a second, it was like I couldn't talk.

She stopped sweeping and wrapped me in her arms while her perfume, a mixture of rain and sea salt, settled over me. "Let's go," she said.

We walked outside and stood on the street that led to our house. The sun sparkled off the ocean in tiny bursts of light.

"Mama." I made my voice as still as I could.

She looked at me carefully, up and down, and then put on her sunglasses.

"Mama, something awful just happened, something that might upset you." My hands started to sweat again, and I wiped them on my skirt. I knew I had to tell her, but at the same time, I thought she would be mad at Daddy because the police had taken him.

Mama turned, looking up the street.

"Mama!" I said louder. "Do you hear me? I need to tell you something awful."

She breathed in deep, the way she does when she is about to tell her opinion on why roses should be sprayed with Listerine mouthwash rather than pesticides because not only did the Listerine keep the aphids off better, it helped grow more flowers.

"Today I saw Daddy being taken away in a police car to jail." I waited to see what she had to say. I thought, *Any minute now and she's gonna roll her eyes and start her speech about always having to fix everything.* But Mama didn't say anything. She just kept looking up the street. I heard her let out a loud sigh, the same one she does after she's read her horoscope for the day and doesn't like what it says. Like she wishes she were a Gemini instead of a Cancer because Gemini is expecting faraway travel or a call from a long-lost friend.

"I don't know what's going on," I said, thinking this was not how she would normally act. "I'm sure it's all a big mistake. We need to help him."

She turned to look at me and took my hands in hers, holding them. I could feel her silver rings on her fingers, and the one aquamarine stone she always wore for good luck. "I know, Groovy," she said finally.

"You know?" I took a step backward, letting her hands drop from mine. I couldn't decide if

I felt surprised, or confused. I hadn't seen her anywhere near the shop where Frankie and I had been sitting when Daddy was driven away in the police car. "How do you know?" I asked.

"Because, baby," she said, "I was the one who called the police."

FIVE-STAR CHOCOLATE-COVERED STRAWBERRIES

Here's the thing about Mama. She does things when she's good and ready. And only *she* decides when she's ready. It didn't matter that I was all wound up and couldn't sit down or breathe normally. Or that she hadn't told me she'd actually had a *plan* to call the police about Daddy.

She walked ten thousand miles an hour up the hill to our house, went right to her room, lit a lavender candle, and pulled her curtains closed.

I stood in her doorway while she lay in bed. The hum of her ceiling fan filled the room, sending drifts of lavender smell in every direction and lifting the bottom of the curtains slightly, as if they were breathing.

"Mama, please, *tell* me what's going on." I waited. "Why would you call the police about Daddy?"

"Shhh, baby," she whispered. "Be quiet. I need to rest." She tucked cucumber slices between the folds of a wet washcloth and then pressed it over her eyes.

"But Mama—"

She held up her hand. "Not now."

"But, Mama, I don't see how *this* is a good time for a beauty treatment. And those cucumbers were for the salad tonight!" I practically yelled the words.

"This is *not* a beauty treatment. This is a stress reliever, for headaches." She breathed deeply, letting out air through her mouth.

"Daddy would never do this," I announced. "He would tell me what's going on."

Mama sat up in bed, the cucumbers spilling

into a pile of green. Her face tightened, and she stared hard into my eyes.

I stepped back into the hallway, sensing her anger. But it didn't stop me from pushing further, and saying the very thing I'd spent months trying not to say. "Like the time he took me to the dog races," I heard myself tell her. "When he told me you were *serious* about wanting him to move out. He told me *everything*. He told me how *you* wanted it and *he* didn't."

Mama pressed her lips tight, like she was trying to control the words that were about to burst out. Then she calmly said, "Like he did today, baby? Like he told you why the police came?"

Tears covered my eyes, making her look blurry.

"As usual, I'm going to have to fix everything," she said. "I'll tell you why I called the police. But not right this second. I don't feel well, and talking makes it worse." She closed her eyes and lay down again.

I watched her inhale and exhale slowly, thinking she would say something else.

Nothing.

I walked to the kitchen, leaving her words behind, and sat at the table. My cooking notebook lay open to the chocolate-covered strawberry recipe I'd made the night before to celebrate Daddy getting his new job at the hardware store. Fifteen perfectly coated strawberries waited on a glass plate for someone to eat them. You could see where two had once been stuck to the plate—the two Daddy and I had taste-tested to make sure I got the recipe right.

"You just might have an aptitude for cooking," he'd told me as he ate the strawberry. "This is good."

"Really?" I'd felt proud.

"Really. I could eat them all." Daddy smiled his smile. The one that said, *You are my favorite girl*.

"The thing about chocolate-covered strawberries is that everyone thinks they're really fancy," I said. "But they're not. They just *look* fancy. So people think they're special."

Daddy inspected his strawberry carefully. "I see what you mean."

"In cooking school, they teach you the exact temperature that chocolate melts. They use a candy thermometer," I told him.

"Well," he said, "these are pretty special."

After he'd left, I'd drawn five stars in my cooking notebook next to my secret recipe of two parts dark chocolate and one part milk chocolate. My personal food critic had said they were the best.

Mama almost never tasted the cakes I made. Not even the extra-moist ones. She said her diets didn't allow for the calories. Plus, she was always in a hurry and didn't have time to sit down the way Daddy and I did.

She'd dash through the kitchen on her way out. It was always the same conversation.

"I see you made another cake," she'd say.

"Chocolate with chocolate frosting," I'd tell her. I truly admired Betty Crocker, all she'd done for cakes, how easy she'd made baking them from a box.

"I wonder what sign Betty Crocker is," Mama said one day. "I bet she's a Pisces."

"Betty Crocker is not a real person, Mama," I told her. "They made her up just so people could write to someone with their baking questions. Somebody even drew a picture of what she would look like. I have it in my cooking notebook." I reached over to my notebook and flipped to the first page, which was where I'd taped her picture.

Mama studied the drawing. "No . . . ," she said after a minute. "She wouldn't have *brown* hair. If she *was* real, she'd look like Barbara Bush."

"More like Martha Washington," I told her.

"Same thing," Mama said. Then she ran her finger across the top of the cake, and licked the frosting off before I could tell her not to.

Sitting in our kitchen with the leftover heat from the oven filling the room, and eating chocolate cake, I would tell Daddy everything. Like my favorite color being white, and how I was going to write a cookbook one day that listed all of my perfect menus for every possible situation—which I was good at coming up with. And even how I was going to be trained at the cooking school in San Francisco when I got older.

I decided on going to cooking school because of what started happening in third grade during lunch recess. Every day kids at my lunch table would look over what I'd brought to eat like it was some new discovery. "What'd you bring today, Groovy?" "You wanna trade your sandwich for my two chocolate cupcakes and one cinnamon applesauce?" "Here, I'll give you all my milk money, plus a bag of chips, and a cookie for that sandwich."

Well, this amazed me because the sandwich isn't even the *good* part of a lunch. It gets eaten last, after the drink and the chips and the pretzels. After the dessert. And then it gets eaten only if people are still really hungry.

But *my* sandwiches became famous that year. *Famous.*

So after Mama told me how good luck really had found me with my great-grandmother leaving a savings account for my future, I'd planned on becoming a real chef. I'd planned on it so much it felt like my true destiny.

And with my favorite color being white, the actual color real chefs wore: It was meant to be.

But Mama said she already knew all those things about me. That mothers had instincts that allowed matters of the heart to transfer automatically without speaking.

Well, why couldn't she understand now why I was so upset?

I finally decided to leave her a note.

> *Mama,*
> *I went to the Swallow. I don't know why you are not talking to me. How are we supposed to be a family if Daddy is in jail?*
> *From,*
> *Your daughter*

Then I headed for the Swallow. Because at least Frankie would be there. And I could tell him what Mama had done. How she had had my daddy *arrested*. And how at any second, one of those stars that Mama consulted in her horoscope each day might come undone from its place in the universe and fall from the sky.

TORTILLAS IN CELLOPHANE WRAP

The bells on the glass door to the Swallow chimed as I pushed it open. Inside the smell of flour tortillas and cinnamon greeted me. Add to that all the onions, peppers, and chilies heating up on the stove, and you could tell it was the kind of place people liked coming to.

"Hey, Groovy," Frankie's stepbrother, Luis, shouted from the back of the store when he saw me. He stood at the counter, chopping ingredients. His height made him look older than he was, and his black hair shone like the night sky. "Come on back here and help me make these tacos. I'm running behind schedule. The ferry driver went home sick, and Frankie's gonna have to bring the boat in for the day. He's at the dock refueling right now."

Luis's biggest moneymaker was not the ferry service he ran back and forth across the harbor for tourists every day, but his secret-recipe tacos passed down from his Aunt Regina. He bought special chilies from Mexico each month when he went to visit her; they were the ingredient no one could guess. The one that made people come back to buy two or three dozen more tacos and a Styrofoam cooler to take them home in.

"Sure," I told him, even though I was disappointed I wouldn't be able to talk to Frankie right away.

"Thanks. I kind of thought you wouldn't mind." He smiled and tossed me the cellophane wrap. "And don't forget to wear the plastic gloves."

I nodded. I knew that after Luis had turned

twenty-one and bought the Swallow Shop & Ferry and the apartment above—where he and Frankie lived—he was determined to make it into a first-rate place. I'd always pictured Luis being a fisherman when he got old enough, like his father. But he'd said it was out of the question. Frankie needed stability and after Frankie's mama had gone and did what she did, Luis was going to do his best to give it to him. The salt would damn well disappear from the ocean before he left Frankie—his very words.

He'd take Frankie to hear Pastor Ken most Sundays at church. "God knows everything you need," Luis told Frankie over and over.

I went along with them to church every so often because I wanted the same for me: everything I needed. Even though Mama stayed behind. She'd say, "Baby, I'm not sure God even knows the color of my hair, and besides, who knows better about what I need than I do?"

I walked over to the food-prep area in the Swallow and washed my hands for exactly sixty seconds, as outlined in the *Joy of Cooking* guidelines for proper kitchen hygiene. I knew the chicken taco recipe by heart, being that Luis had finally told it to me after me begging him for months. And I mean begging, because according to Luis, secret family recipes were secret.

"Always use the yellow chilies," he'd told me. "That's the secret."

So I'd taped an exact picture of what the chilies looked like in the margin of page 14 in my cooking notebook where I'd written the recipe. There were recipes I'd made up myself in that notebook, but most were from other people. Some were clipped from magazines like *Vogue* and *Harper's Bazaar*, which technically weren't cooking magazines but were the only ones Mama got. Things like "Ten-Minute Meals" and "Fast, Easy Dinners," which I suppose is the type of cooking ladies who read those magazines do. Like Mama.

Me and Daddy were food people, though. We'd go to the market together, walk through the aisles, and get inspiration. Once we came across a breadfruit. I had no idea what recipe a breadfruit would go into. Neither did Daddy.

The store owner said, "Got those breadfruits from a farm in Hawaii yesterday. Be great in a bacon-and-milk gumbo, don't you think?"

We nodded at him. Like we cooked breadfruit all the time, and in fact, breadfruit was growing in our garden at home this very minute.

Luis yelled from the front of the store, "And, Groovy, we had an order for ten cheese enchiladas to be picked up this afternoon at four. Please start those, too, if you can. The recipe's on top of the microwave."

"Okay," I yelled back. "In cooking school, they teach you to make two or three dishes at the same time, like they do in professional restaurants. They call it kitchen management."

Luis leaned back around the counter and smiled. "Maybe I should take that class," he said.

I smiled back at him. Just being inside the Swallow made me feel calmer. Putting together the tacos with the chicken and cheese and onion and chilies, making something perfect with my hands, made me feel like a different person.

Maybe it was because I appreciated each ingredient by itself—the way it smelled, the way the onions always made me cry when I cut them, even if I lit a candle to absorb the fumes the way they did on TV. It didn't matter, I still cried.

It was Luis who taught me to chop onions. I figured out the dicing part so fast and easy that he said I was a natural. Those were his exact words: "Groovy, you are a natural at chopping onions."

The Swallow was the only place I really got to cook. Luis said he was happy to have the help. Plus, we didn't always have the ingredients I needed at home. I could never talk Mama into buying extras like cinnamon or fancy cheeses. But Luis's shop had everything.

It was named after the birds that fly each year to the Mission that was built by Junípero Serra in San Juan Capistrano. In the old days of California, the padres had walked north from Mexico and built missions to spread the good news about Jesus and teach the Indians new ways to farm.

After the mission in San Juan Capistrano was built, the swallows flew there each spring and made little mud nests to raise their babies in after they hatched. People say there used to be so many birds in the sky, it became dark while they flew over the streets to their destination. If you didn't look up, you might think it was an eclipse.

Frankie says it's fitting that they call Luis's store the Swallow Shop & Ferry because the birds will be coming to the area long after we're gone.

"Frankie, why do you love those birds so much?" Luis would ask him each year when they returned.

And Frankie would always say the same thing: "Because I can count on them."

ORANGE-FLAVORED TUMS

The second I finished wrapping up those tacos and making the ten cheese enchiladas, I ran to the dock in front of the Swallow. Its worn gray wood was as soft as an old pair of cotton pajamas, from years of sun and salt and people walking on it. In the distance I could see the fog building like a wall of dark mist, pushing at high speed toward us. Frankie was tying the ferry to the pier posts good and tight with slipknots, the same kind they use in the navy.

"Frankie," I said. "It's Mama's fault my daddy's in jail."

"Your mother's fault? Why?" His face was a mixture of 50 percent surprise and 40 percent that-can't-be right, and 10 percent something else that I couldn't quite make out.

"I don't know. She won't talk about it. She came down with a bad headache right after she told me she was the one who called the police." I felt tears in my eyes again. "She's at home. She said, and I quote, 'I don't feel well, and talking makes it worse.' " I shook my head.

Frankie frowned. "You'll have to get her to tell you what happened." He looked me over good and sighed. Then he said, "But I'm sort of not surprised."

I looked at the ground. It was the first time Frankie had actually *said* something like this. But I knew he thought it from time to time because he would stop himself in the middle of a sentence sometimes when we talked about my daddy. He would say, "Do you think your dad—?" and then he would stop. And I would say, "What?" And he would say, "Nothing."

And then it felt weird between us. So Frankie would quickly change the subject and use this cheerful voice that really didn't sound like him.

"So what are you saying?" I looked up at Frankie.

He shook his head. "That she'll have to tell you sooner or later. I mean, he is your father."

I nodded. He was right.

Frankie pulled the blue tarps over the ferry and worked to secure the bumpers. "Help me tie these ropes tight. The weather's coming in and I wanna get the boat cleaned off and covered."

"Okay." I grabbed the lines and did my best with the knots. "I'm just saying, I don't know what he could've done to make her call the police."

Frankie shrugged. I could tell he didn't want to talk about it anymore. I watched him wind the rope ends into a perfect coil on the dock. Then he reached for the hose and started spraying off the tarp.

A small boy with dark brown hair, who looked like he might be in kindergarten, ran up to us.

"My sister's *not* gonna like you getting water all over her masterpiece," he said, glaring at the sidewalk in front of him. A large chalk drawing of a bird flying over a tree, similar to the one I'd seen earlier, covered the cement. The claws of the bird were twice the size of the boy's tennis shoes.

Mist from Frankie's hose was drifting in his direction, making the air look as if it were shining, each atom lit up and falling lightly over the drawing.

I walked over to him. I hadn't noticed the drawing before, but there it was, signed by Marisol Cruz, who was in my grade at school. The way she'd shaded the bird's wings and eyes, it was easy to see how much she loved birds.

"She'll be here any minute and she's not gonna like it," the boy told me.

Frankie turned off the hose right away. "Sorry," he said. "Who are you?"

"Felix," he told us.

"Are you supposed to be here by yourself?" Frankie asked him.

"My sister's coming. I'm not gonna be by myself. She let me carry her chalk box. I'm not gonna drop it." He held up a white cardboard box covered in construction-paper drawings: a bird standing, a bird flying, a bird nesting.

"Okay," Frankie said. "Just so long as you're not by yourself."

"Marisol drew this swallow. She's gonna open up a real art gallery. She's gonna get her pictures in magazines and newspapers. That's what she said." Felix opened the top of the box and took out a piece of blue chalk, holding it up. "Black is her favorite color. Mine is sky-blue. She said I could color the sky for her birds, so long as I don't go over her lines. Otherwise, I can't be her assistant anymore. Assistants have to do what they're told."

"The fog is coming in fast today!" Luis called to Frankie and me from the shop. He stood looking over the ocean, his black hair blowing in the breeze. "Come inside, you two. It almost feels like rain."

It was true. Fog had rolled in on top of us and curled around the sides of the boat where it touched the sea. It was the same fog that brought rust and mildew to everyone's roses except Mama's, and was so famous up in the San Francisco area that photos of it made covers of calendars. And postcards.

Beads of water were busy forming on the outside of my clothes and in my hair, making it curly and frizzy. I knew Mama hated this kind of dampness because she said it ruined a good hair-straightening job.

We hurried into the shop just as Marisol found her little brother.

"Sorry about getting water on your drawing!" Frankie yelled to her.

Marisol looked confused. I saw Felix's arms open wide like he was explaining. "I seen the whole thing," I heard him tell her.

Inside the shop, we sat at the rear counter on orange vinyl swivel seats, the kind that turn all the way around with a good push.

Frankie got us Frescas and quesadillas made with three kinds of cheese.

"Frankie!" Luis yelled from the front of the shop. He was getting ready to lock up for the day. "You got some mail yesterday. It's on the counter by the microwave. And, Groovy, your mother called. I told her I'd send you home when you got back."

"Okay," I answered, thinking that her headache must have gotten better by now, and how I wanted to get home ASAP.

I picked up the letter and handed it to Frankie.

He looked at it and gave it back right away. "Throw it in the trash!" he demanded. "I don't want it."

"What is it?" I looked at the front of the envelope but before I could read it, Frankie grabbed it from my hands and tore the letter into pieces, throwing them like bits of confetti onto the terracotta floor.

He stood for a couple of seconds looking at

the ripped-up letter, then took a roll of Tums from his pocket. He unwrapped it past a lemon- and a lime-flavored tablet until he found an orange one, and put it in his mouth. He chewed fast, swallowed, stuffed his hands in his pockets.

"What?" I asked him.

He opened his mouth, then shut it.

Turned around.

Walked out the door.

I knelt down and pushed the tiny pieces of paper into a pile with my hands.

"Leave them there," Luis said as he walked to the back where I was. "He won't read it even when it was in one piece."

We stood real quiet for a minute. I handed the torn-up letter to Luis.

"I knew it was from his mother by the handwriting," he said. "And I didn't know how to tell him when it came yesterday, so I left it on the counter hoping he'd see it and open it. It's the second one he's gotten in three weeks. Before then, nothing. Except those postcards last year. All of a sudden, it's like the Pony Express around here."

Luis opened his hand and the pieces fell slowly into the round cutout in the counter. The same one where customers threw away their used napkins and thin white papers that cover straws. Things nobody thought twice about.

BLUE FLIP-FLOPS
REALLY WORN DOWN

Frankie held anything that had to do with his mother so tight inside that it made him sick— nothing serious, but still, sick. At first the doctors said he had allergies. Then it was headaches. Later they decided it was a sensitive stomach. All of which were wrong, if you ask me. It was just plain sadness. That, and maybe him being mad for so long. Because when his mother and stepfather left to fish in the southern waters where the big catches are, they left Frankie behind with his stepbrother, Luis, for what was supposed to be a couple of weeks. Three at the most.

It turned out to be two years with nothing but postcards promising they'd be back as soon as they could.

So far, he was still waiting.

Why she left him was a mystery, and I mean *mystery*. Frankie says the day she left, she only packed enough clothes for a week. In only one suitcase. And it was a small suitcase, like a carry-on, like she really was going to come back.

I knew if she ever did come back for Frankie, it would take a hundred years of explaining before Frankie understood her side. He was just like that. Even with little things. It could take him a whole week to call back if I told him even the tiniest white lie. I'd say, "Frankie, I'm very sorry. I won't do it again. Can we forget about it?"

He never did.

I went outside to look for Frankie. The late-afternoon fog glowed yellow-green around a fluorescent light mounted to the pier. Moisture stuck to everything, a layer of cool wetness.

Marisol and Felix stood side by side, their heads tipped in the same direction. They were looking at Marisol's drawing as though it were a famous painting on display.

She turned around when she heard me.

"It took me a while to fix this one." Marisol pointed to the swallow Frankie had accidentally sprayed with hose water. "Maybe you should be more careful next time. People like to enjoy my drawings, you know. Especially my swallow series."

"The swallows are coming back soon," Felix said.

"It was an accident," I told her. "We didn't see it."

Marisol rolled her eyes. "Right," she said.

"Maybe you should think about drawing somewhere not so close to water," I told her.

"This is where everyone comes to walk. This is where my audience is," she said.

"Your audience is at the restaurant, too," Felix said to his sister. "That's what you told

Dad." Then he turned to me. "My dad is framing Marisol's swallows for the customers at his restaurant to look at. Marisol says they can enjoy her artwork while they eat."

Marisol smiled proudly. "I'm starting out there. Soon I'll be in galleries."

"Oh," I said. "I better go. I'm looking for Frankie."

"Yeah, he walked by here. He didn't even say hello. Or sorry." She waved her hand in the direction of the jetty. "He's out there."

"Thanks," I said, walking away as fast as I could. Marisol Cruz wasn't the nicest girl; we found that out pretty quick when she moved here last year with her father, who opened up a Mexican restaurant in town. And the fact that she sat alone at lunch recess, sketching every day, made it even harder to get to know her.

I knew where Frankie would be, without Marisol's help. I found him sitting on the jetty rocks that overlooked the ocean.

Mr. Tom was sitting with his guitar next to

Frankie. He played a song I'd heard before but couldn't remember the name of.

Mr. Tom didn't live anywhere we knew. Sometimes we saw him sitting on the yellow bench in front of the Swallow when it wasn't too busy, but mostly he kept to himself. He had a cardboard box of old sea charts, and a red umbrella that he slept under so he wouldn't get dropped on by the seagulls. His face was a storm of lines and wrinkles, showing the long journeys he'd been on.

Frankie said that Mr. Tom knew the way to the islands off the coast without using a GPS. And that he was waiting for a free boat ride to take him there so he could retire.

I walked up to them and stood listening to the song.

After a while I said, "Luis told me you got another letter from your mother a couple of weeks ago, Frankie. Why didn't you tell me?" I sat down next to him, away from Mr. Tom, on account of Mama telling me he was crazy.

"I don't want to know what she has to say," Frankie told me.

"I think you should read her letter, though."

"No, thanks," he answered quickly.

"Where was the letter sent from?"

Frankie turned away and shook his head. "I don't care where it was sent from," he said.

Mr. Tom sang on, like he was playing for a huge audience, about a levy and pie. He wore a purple cap over his gray hair and a yellow foul-weather coat, one that had the name Skip Harris embroidered on the left side below the collar. I guessed he'd probably found the coat, being that his name wasn't Skip.

His fingernails were dirty, and long for a man. He wore blue flip-flops that were worn down to nothing. I could see a wad of gray chewed-up gum stuck to the bottom of his right sole. From the grayness of it, I decided it had probably been spearmint-flavored at one time.

Mr. Tom didn't seem to mind me staring at him. He just looked straight ahead and kept singing his words, the fog making his voice sound close and faraway at the same time.

And I thought that if Daddy were here, he would know the words because it sounded like just the kind of music he used to play on his radio. Soft and a little sad.

"Frankie," I said, "why don't you want to know what she has to say? Maybe she *wants* to explain. Unlike *my* mama right now. A letter is a lot different than a postcard."

"I have my own life," he told me. "With Luis." He unwrapped his roll of Tums to the last one. It was lime-flavored, but he ate it anyway.

I watched his face and saw a funny look on it. And I thought it must have taken a lot for him to hide that away for so long because just then, he looked a lot different from the friend I knew who could do anything. I started wishing I had a plate of warm chocolate chip cookies to offer him. Ones that came straight from the oven, something to make him feel better.

Mr. Tom stopped singing. He put his guitar

down and stood up next to Frankie, stretching his arms and hands out with his fingers wide. "You gotta forgive, boy," he told him, "otherwise you keep that with you, like one of those houses they put sandbags around to keep the floodwaters out. Nothin' comes in, but nothin' goes out either."

Frankie looked up at Mr. Tom. He didn't answer him, but I could tell there was something he wanted to say by the way his eyes looked all serious.

"You don't wanna be stuck," Mr. Tom said. "It's only a matter of pride." He let out a long sigh. Then he said, "I've seen this before. Sailors I served with who'd rather stay angry than forgive. And all that personal suffering that comes from built-up anger. It makes no sense, but they'd rather suffer."

Then he took off his knit cap and his yellow coat and started moving his hands in small circles slowly in the air around Frankie.

He started at the top of his shoulders, and made his way to the bottom of Frankie's legs, but without touching him. His eyes were closed tight, like he was feeling for the anger that must have been coming off Frankie that very moment.

And when he came to the bottom of Frankie's tennis shoes, he shook his hands out three times. Like a person does who has no towel to dry them after a good washing.

Then he picked up his guitar with his coat and cap and walked up the hill without looking back, like it never even happened.

WHAT FRANKIE DID WHEN HE TOOK THE DINGHY OUT

I told Frankie that taking Luis's dinghy out at this time of day was a bad idea. I said, "The fog is still coming in. It's practically dark. Luis will wonder where you are." Things like that.

But Frankie kept walking real fast toward the end of the dock, ignoring me, and then stepped into the blue dinghy Luis kept tied up there.

"Where are you going anyway?" I said as I caught up to him, noticing that people were bringing their boats *in* for the day.

At the sound of my voice, Marisol and Felix

looked up from Marisol's drawing.

Frankie reached back to pull the starter cord on the engine. "Can you throw me the line?" he asked, with his arm stretched out to catch it.

I waited for him to answer my question. Puffs of smoke rose from behind the engine while the smell of gasoline looped around us.

Finally he said, "I'm just going for a ride." He extended his arm out farther then, like he was saying, *Okay, now will you throw me the line? I told you what you wanted to know.*

"You're going for a ride? Out there?" Felix asked as he walked up to us. He looked into the distance. His hands and knees were covered in light-blue chalk dust.

"Yeah," Frankie told him.

"Maybe I'll come too," I heard myself say. I untied the rope from the pier post and tossed it to him. Even though I wanted to get home and talk to Mama more than anything, I didn't want to leave Frankie alone. I knew he'd never actually tell me what was wrong, but if I looked close enough, I could see it sometimes. I could see it by the way he'd squint into the air, looking at nothing—which meant he did not agree with what someone said. Or by the way he'd turn and walk away in the middle of a conversation. You knew he was real upset then. I figured him getting into the boat and wanting to leave had to do with what Mr. Tom had said.

Frankie shrugged. "Fine," he told me, slowly backing the boat away from the dock. "You coming or not?"

I glanced out at the fog skimming the top of the sea.

"Can I come too?" Felix asked.

"No, you cannot go with them out there in this weather, Felix Cruz," Marisol said as she stomped toward us and ushered her brother away in a hurry. Like we were common criminals on a crime spree, and before long Felix would be spraying things with hose water and taking boat rides in the fog just because he'd associated with us.

The dinghy inched farther away as Frankie impatiently pressed the motor.

"Wait!" I yelled. "I'm coming."

He reversed the boat and brought it alongside the dock. "Put your life vest on," he told me as I stepped inside.

He waited while I strapped my vest around my waist and sat down on the bench opposite him. Then we picked up speed as Frankie steered us toward the open ocean.

"You gonna wear *your* life vest?" I yelled to him.

He shrugged.

"So where are we going?" I gripped my seat.

Frankie made a fast left turn, carving a capital letter C in the water. "To the far end of the jetty. There's something I need to get."

I pictured the line of huge black rocks stacked high on top of one another to keep the big waves and swells from hitting our dock. And I wondered what he would need to get there.

We raced along, our dinghy rising and falling

with the crest of the tide. Foamy sprays of cold water splashed over the sides onto our tennis shoes while the fog built a thick wall around us. I held on so tight to my seat that my hands became stuck in a holding-on position.

If you think the ocean looks nice and peaceful from shore, well, then you haven't been on it while the fog rolls in.

Frankie said he'd never seen it this dark for it still technically being daytime. I said the shadows on the water looked just like shark fins.

When we finally got to the far end of the jetty, he shut the motor off, and our dinghy scratched against the huge jagged rocks. Bits of uprooted seaweed swirled next to us in the water. Seagulls flew from their usual spot on the boulders at the sound of us nearing.

Frankie stepped out and quickly tied the dinghy to a pointed rock. "Bail some of that water out," he told me, pointing to the bottom of the boat.

"I'm not getting out," I said. In the distance,

I heard the foghorn warning boaters to be careful.

"I'll be right back then," he told me.

I nodded. "Hurry."

I waited.

I pulled my life vest tighter.

I wished I hadn't come.

I decided to bail water, but no matter how much water I threw out, it never seemed to get lower than the tops of my shoelaces. I thought, *There's a hole in the boat. The ocean is seeping in. It's going to sink. Come on, Frankie. Hurry.*

Leave it to the late-afternoon-turning-to-night fog to play all kinds of tricks on your eyes. Because I was pretty sure I saw an enormous sea lion swim by. One with huge flippers. And I imagined him smashing the dinghy with one of them and sending it onto its side.

So I counted the blasts from the foghorn to keep me from thinking about that sea lion and his flippers.

A million minutes later, when I'd counted all

the way to thirty-six, Frankie came back holding a smallish green metal box about the size of a brick. He quickly stepped into the dinghy with it and started the motor. "I thought you were going to bail the water out," he told me.

"I tried. But it didn't work. What's that?" I asked, looking at the metal box.

He ran his hand along the top of the box as the dinghy waited for him to steer it home. Then he reached into his pocket and took out a black stone just smaller than the box. When he opened the box, I could see postcards inside. The top one read, *Greetings from Mexico*, with a picture of a smiling sun on it. "They're postcards from my mother," he told me. "I've been keeping them here, buried under the big rock by the red warning buoy. Every time I'd get a postcard, I'd bring it out here and put it in this box."

I watched as he placed the black stone on top of the pile of postcards and closed the box tight.

"How many are in there?" I said.

"Not many."

"Why'd you put the stone inside?"

"So it will sink," he said. Then he steered us toward the shore so fast that I slipped back on my seat.

For a long time, neither of us said anything. I squinted into the gray damp air as the dinghy bounced across the water, making its way home. I tried to think of things to say that might help so he wouldn't be so mad at his mama.

When Frankie cut the motor, we were almost back to the dock. I couldn't see it through the fog, but I heard shore sounds echoing off the top of the water. Boat halyards. Engines. A dad yelling for his boy.

"Why'd you stop?" I asked him. "We're almost back. Come on, Frankie, let's go."

"Just a minute," he told me.

The smell of salt and clamshells rose up around us as I watched him lean over the side of the dinghy. He looked deep into the ocean for a long time, like he was making sure it was a good spot.

Then he held the metal box with the postcards

from his mama inside, and the black stone that would make sure it sank, over the sea, over the spot he'd been looking at for so long.

And he quickly dropped it into the amber green-gray water, like a person does who drops a penny off a tall building. Like he couldn't wait to see it disappear.

FISH STICKS

I found a note on the kitchen table from Mama when I got home. I stood in damp tennis shoes reading it.

> *Dear Groovy,*
> *I waited for you to come back until 6:00. I had to run to the salon for an appointment, but I will be back soon. Wait here. We need to have a talk.*
>
> > *—Mama*

I crumpled the note into a wad and threw it into the corner of the room, mad I'd missed her. The note unfolded slowly, bit by bit, like it was trying to be read again. Like it was saying, *Are you sure you don't want to have a second look? There might be a secret code in here, or something you didn't see the first time.*

But I ignored it and walked into the living room.

With Saturday being Mama's usual late day at the salon—in order to fit in her clients who had to work during the week—I had plenty of time to wait for her to tell me what was going on.

But waiting is the hardest thing anyone ever has to do. You think you can just sit and let time go by. Well, no. Because that is exactly when time does *not* go by. You look at the clock and think, *Surely it has been ten minutes by now*, when it has only been one or two.

So I dusted the furniture.

I arranged yellow roses from the garden in a glass on the table.

I wiped up the crumbs on the countertop in the kitchen, the ones that fell from the toaster.

I decided to use extreme kindness and politeness with her when she got home. The kind Mama said they use in Louisiana.

I checked my cooking notebook for ideas. I am here to tell you that I made the best dinner I could think of because I am good at coming up with the exact right food for every situation.

Say you are needing to tell your parents about a worse-than-normal grade you got on a test. I have a recipe for that: macaroni and cheese. Or say you are wanting to ask for something new, like a pair of tennis shoes. I have a recipe for that: French toast with whipped cream.

But if you know you'll more than likely be listening to bad news, then I have a whole menu for that: Gorton's frozen fish sticks with creamed corn and milk.

After I cooked it all, I set everything out on our hardly-ever-used best plates.

And when I stepped back from the dinner

table, I thought it looked perfect. Arranged fine enough to get anyone to tell the facts.

I stood by the front door so I could watch for her. Tiny silverfish bugs scattered from under the doormat. The smell of salt drifted in from the ocean on a nighttime breeze that made the roses along the fence bend slightly sideways, like they were reaching their necks to see Mama walk up the street like I was.

After forever, I saw her coming, carrying her black bag of beauty supplies. The ones we got for free to try and then report back to the salon owner on how well they made our hair shine, or how strong our ends became after just one washing.

"Hi, Mama," I said, real sweet, as she walked up the sidewalk. "I made dinner for us so you wouldn't have to cook. I tried to think about other people like you tell me to. I thought you would be hungry." I stepped aside from the front door, letting her walk in before me.

She dropped her bag of supplies onto the couch and sat down to take off her high heels.

She looked tired.

"Thanks, baby," she said, "but I thought we'd go out for dinner tonight."

I looked at the table and hoped she would notice all the trouble I went to. She followed my eyes to the kitchen and saw how I had set everything out. But it didn't seem to matter. Instead she got up and said, "I'll take a quick bath and then we'll go, all right?"

"But, Mama," I answered, "I already made dinner."

She turned and walked down the hall to her bathroom.

"Why did you call the police?" I blurted out, knowing my plan had failed, leaving extreme kindness behind.

She stopped. And for a second, I thought she would tell me by the way she looked so long at the carpet.

"I have a right to know." I took a step toward her, but her eyes met mine and stopped me.

"I just walked in, Groovy, and it's been a *very*

long day." She pulled her sweater over her head and nodded. "But you're right. You need to know. I'll be out in a few minutes." Then she pulled the door shut quietly, like she was tired of arguing and had no more strength.

I slumped onto the couch.

I waited.

I could hear the water running in the bathroom. Tears settled into the corners of my eyes.

I wanted to run after Mama and tell her that she had no right to send Daddy away. I wanted to grab her by the arm and make her explain it to me. I wanted to throw the dinner and yellow roses into the trash.

I wanted to yell.

But I knew she would only become angry with me. Like she did when Daddy would try to force her to see things his way.

So I decided I would do whatever it took to get her to tell me what had happened. If she would rather go out to dinner, that would be fine with me.

OUR USUAL TABLE BY THE FIRE PIT

A million minutes later Mama came out.

I jumped up quick from the couch. "Ready to go?" I looked at her face, trying to read her, but determined to get my way this time.

"Yep." She picked up her purse.

"Do you wanna call ahead for a table?" I asked.

"Nope."

"Shouldn't we clean up the dishes first?"

"Later, baby," she told me.

"Fine," I told her.

She stopped in the doorway and looked me over. "You're going to wear that?"

I checked my outfit. Skirt, T-shirt, tennis shoes. It seemed okay. "Yes," I answered, like maybe I wasn't going to after all. "Why, should I change?" I wondered how she could notice what I wore at a time like this.

"No," she said in her voice that really meant yes. "I guess you're fine."

We walked down the hill toward José's Cantina, Marisol's father's restaurant. The fog was even thicker than before. If I squinted, I could see it rolling like little tumbleweeds across the street, moving like it was in a hurry to get somewhere.

I thought about Daddy and knew that if he were here with me as we walked blind through the fog with practically no visibility, and under emotional distress at the same time, he'd put his arm around me and say, "Don't worry, Groovy. I'm right here." Just like he did whenever I woke up from a bad dream when I was younger. He'd sit with me until I fell asleep again. I'd say, "Daddy, tell me about the day I was born." And he'd tell it like it happened just yesterday, like it had been the best day ever in the whole history of the world.

"I've been thinking, baby," Mama said loudly in a happyish voice.

I looked up at her, surprised at her tone after our talk at home.

"You know those big strawberries you make for special occasions? The ones covered in chocolate like you made yesterday?" she asked.

"Yes."

"Well, every time you make those, they look so beautiful. I feel like a queen when I eat one." Mama stopped and sighed. She watched the fog rolling quietly in our path.

I could almost *see* the inside of her head working, coming up with some kind of a plan right there, and I wondered what this had to do with Daddy.

"Anyway"—she shrugged and started walking again—"I was thinking that, well, it might be nice if you started making those chocolate-covered strawberries more often."

"But they're for special occasions. Like birthdays." I didn't mention Daddy probably not having his new job anymore.

"Well, it's someone's birthday every day, Groovy. Look in the horoscope section of the newspaper and you can clearly see that."

"But I don't know those people. Why would I make them strawberries?"

"You could *sell* the strawberries, baby. You could make up a nice batch every now and then and ask Luis to sell them for you. I'm sure he'd do that. People would love your strawberries."

"I guess."

"Groovy." Mama stopped and looked at me. "You could start saving the money you made for later, when you need it. For something special." She nodded and then started walking again.

"I'll think about it," I said. But I knew right away exactly what I would save for. Mama was right. Even with the savings account Great-grandmother had left for my future, cooking school would probably be expensive. Not to mention I'd need chef's knives, aprons with my name written on them, and white bakery hats. The kind that stand tall and high in the shape of an oval. I decided maybe I *could* sell chocolate-covered strawberries.

"It's just an idea," Mama said. And then quietly added, "You never know when things can change. It's good to be prepared."

I looked over at her. "What do you mean?"

"Never mind," she said.

When we got to José's Cantina, we were the only ones there besides three tourists sitting at the bar. They were drinking sodas and talking loudly about how when a storm system comes in from offshore like this, the coastal weather is completely unpredictable and dangerous for boaters. I heard them say they were going to have to spend the night in town until the weather cleared up.

"Here for dinner kinda late," Marisol said when she saw us. She walked toward us from the kitchen. Felix was right behind her, carrying two paper cups with straws sticking out of the tops. "Need a table?"

"Thank you," Mama told her.

I didn't say anything to her on purpose.

"Here you go," Marisol said, waving toward the back of the restaurant.

Mama and I sat at our usual table by the fire pit, where the restaurant roasted whole chickens and green onions. I started eating the corn chips and salsa the busboy brought us while Mama lit the red candle in the middle of our table. Pictures of swallows hung on every wall. Flocks of swallows, swallows perched on houses, swallows in olive trees.

"Well, see ya," Marisol told us.

"See ya," Felix said. He raised his hand to wave good-bye but then stopped so he wouldn't spill the sodas he was holding.

Marisol rolled her eyes and left. Felix hurried behind her. "I have your drink, Marisol," he called.

After a while I said to Mama, "So, we're here now." Which really translated to, *I'm waiting patiently but I'm not feeling patient anymore.*

The waitress walked over and stood next to our table.

"We'll have two virgin strawberry margaritas," Mama told the waitress. "And ask the bartender to use the fresh strawberries, not the frozen mix." She smiled real nice then, to be sure to get her way. I knew she never drank alcohol, in order to keep toxins out of her body and all.

"Well," Mama said after the waitress brought our drinks, "I'm sure you want me to tell you the reason I called the police about your father."

I looked up right away. "Yes."

Mama breathed in deeply and then motioned for the waitress to come back. She told her that we would be a while before we ordered our dinner and would she please mind giving us some privacy in the meantime.

The waitress shrugged her shoulders and

started to walk away. Which probably translated to she'd rather not have to take our order anyway.

Mama thanked her and turned to me.

I could tell she was ready to tell me something very important by the way she straightened up in her seat and arranged her fork and knife perfectly on the table next to her plate.

"But before I can tell you about your father," she said, "I have to tell you the *whole* story of your great-grandmother. The original Eleanor Robinson."

FLASHLIGHTS AND CHOCOLATE BARS

"She was an Aquarius," Mama said, like that would explain it all. "Creative and intellectual. She slept past noon every day, and collected small porcelain statues of owls because they were creatures of the night—something she was always studying." She leaned in close across the table to tell me more about my great-grandmother.

I knew Mama had always thought of her as being someone very special, because she named me after her.

"Well, you know she wrote science fiction novels," Mama told me. "But you might not know how extraordinary she was. For example, she only worked after midnight. Usually until four A.M. She said it was the best time to write because people did and said things then that they normally wouldn't in the daytime. From her apartment window in New York, she could watch all kinds of people passing through the night. She even thought she saw paranormal events from time to time."

"What do you mean?" I asked.

"Events that don't normally happen. Things that can't be explained, Groovy. Like that time last year when the entire crew of the *Lovely Anna* disappeared. The harbor patrol said they had set a course for home, but they never made it. It was a huge mystery."

Mama kept talking and as she did, her story started to sound like one of those that camp counselors tell around a fire after dinner. When everyone is tucked away in their sleeping bags with flashlights and chocolate bars, wearing their pajamas.

Her face glowed from the light of the red candle on the table, and the smoke from the flame rose up around her in little gray wisps and then disappeared into the air.

"What does this have to do with Daddy?" I said, trying to keep her on track.

"Well." She dabbed her mouth with her napkin. "I'm getting to it. You see, your great-grandmother was very smart. She had so many books stacked up along the walls of her apartment that it was hard to walk without accidentally kicking over a pile of them. Some of the piles were as high as the top of my head. She always said that good writers are even better readers, and she was a great reader. She probably liked reading better than talking to most people."

Mama looked out through the window, and stared into the fog for a moment. I could see her being careful not to knock over one of those stacks of books as she walked through the memory of Great-grandmother's apartment.

But her most favorite books were those

written by Isaac Asimov," Mama said, and she turned back again to look at me. "She read those over and over. She kept them in a special pile by themselves. I remember she used to read to me from that pile when I visited her."

Mama stopped talking and put her napkin on the table. She smoothed out the wrinkles she had made while holding it on her lap, over and over with the palm of her hand, like it was suddenly very important that her napkin was completely, 100 percent wrinkle-free. She breathed in deep, and for a minute I thought I might be in trouble for something I did, from the look on her face.

"What's wrong, Mama?"

"Groovy . . . this brings me to the part about you and your father." She made sure I was listening good, and I was. I knew she was finally going to tell me what I wanted to know.

"Your great-grandmother left to you *Foundation*, written by Mr. Asimov. A first edition from the year 1951. She came out to see you after you were born and gave it to me. I have been keeping it for you in a box filled with all of her unfinished stories, which she also left to you. There are pages and pages of her writing in that box. I was waiting until you were older to give them to you, so you would be able to take good care of them."

Mama stopped and took my hands in hers, rubbing her thumbs over my knuckles real slow and frowning just a little. Her lips were pushed tight together and she had wrinkles between her eyes.

"Mama, please, what are you saying?"

"You see, Groovy," she said, "the first Eleanor Robinson, being the emotional type, was so touched to have someone named after her that she passed along her most prized possessions to you. She knew you would know what to do with them, being that you have the same name," Mama explained.

I wasn't sure why she was acting so strange and ignoring my questions about Daddy.

Mama looked straight at me then. "Groovy,

you know she left some money to you, but I've never told you how much it was. I wanted to wait until you got older and were ready to go to college."

I nodded. "I know, Mama. I told you, I'm going to use it for cooking school. I have it all planned out."

Mama looked down at her plate. She pressed her fingers to her forehead like she suddenly felt a sharp pain. Then she said, "It was twenty-five thousand dollars, baby. All the money she had."

I looked at Mama in shock, and she looked back at me. My mouth dropped open and Mama just kept nodding, like she was trying to believe it too. Neither one of us could say anything.

I'd never known anyone who had twenty-five thousand dollars. I couldn't imagine where all that money would fit. And I thought that my great-grandmother must have been a really good writer to save up all that money.

Then after a real long time of looking at each other with amazement, and all this can-you-believe-it feeling in the air between us, she said, "Well, should we order now? They must be getting ready to close up the place soon." And she motioned for the waitress to come over to our table with the most everyday, normal look on her face. Like she had just told me something about the weather, or what was on special at the market.

TWO SPECIALS TO GO

We sat at that table for a long time waiting for the waitress to come. So long that I could feel the backs of my legs getting indentations from the wicker chair. Mama pressed her lips tight and kept staring at me. It was as if she was trying to decide something.

Me, I am embarrassed to admit that with the news Mama told me . . . I felt a smallish wave of hope flood into a corner of my brain, unexpectedly of course, about my future. It came quick, surprising me that I could think about myself, so selfishly, at a time when everything bad was happening to Daddy. The thought got bigger and bigger, until finally it was the only thing I could think: I would actually definitely be able to go to cooking school when I got older because I could *pay for it*. I was sure twenty-five thousand dollars would be enough. Yes, I could sell my chocolate-covered strawberries if I wanted to, like Mama'd suggested, but I already had enough money without doing that.

I would learn how to dice vegetables without lifting the top of the knife off the cutting board, like they do on TV, and use a real flaming kitchen torch, and make pastry cream that comes out all fancy from a bag. I would use a zester to make the skin of lemons float off like confetti onto the tops of pies and cookies.

I would write a cookbook, listing my perfect menus for every situation, the ones I'd copied into my notebook.

I looked at the floor to keep Mama from noticing the tiny grin of happiness I couldn't hold back anymore.

But Mama let out a loud breath and stood up, like she'd read my thoughts. She waved at the waitress. "Can we have two specials to go, please?" she yelled across the room to her.

"Why are we leaving?" I stood up with her.

The waitress nodded and hurried back to the kitchen, stuffing her order pad into the front pocket of her apron.

"I think we should run by the salon." Mama started walking toward the cashier. She reached for her wallet deep inside her purse. Her makeup bag dropped to the tile floor as her hands fumbled inside. Lipsticks spun out in half circles, their silver cases twinkling as they caught the light. Eyeliners and compacts and mascaras scattered.

"But we haven't eaten dinner. And it's practically *midnight*." I watched her stuff her things back into her bag, like she was racing against time, like we were practicing a drill at school and had to leave our classroom while the emergency bell rang loudly in bursts of three over the intercom.

"You need a deep conditioning," she told me.

"Your hair looks dry. Plus, you're way overdue to have your bangs trimmed."

I stopped in my tracks. "What's wrong, Mama?" I knew her idea for fixing any problem was a deep-conditioning hair treatment. It was used as a cure-all for emotional problems; or female stresses, the monthly type that ladies sometimes had; or illnesses; or as a pick-me-up for really, *really* bad days. The last time she'd insisted on giving me one was the day Daddy'd lost a job he'd kept for almost a year.

She paid the cashier quickly and picked up the paper bag that held our dinners, thin ribbons of hot steam streamed behind her as she walked out the door. "Come on, Groovy."

"I'm not going," I told her as I ran to catch up, but only to protest. "Tell me what's wrong. I know something's wrong, Mama. And by the way, I am *not* getting my hair done." I stood my ground, watching her walk up the street.

But Mama kept going. "Hurry up," she yelled over her shoulder. "It's getting late."

Anger rose inside me. I ran to catch up. Her body was like a magnet, and I couldn't help myself from being pulled into her path of explanations.

I knew her words might disappear into the fog if I wasn't there to grab hold of them while I could.

IN FRONT OF THE MERMAID

The smell of mangoes and peppermint filled the air at the salon, as I sat there with my hair wrapped tight in a mound of white towels. Mama had rubbed her favorite special-reserve conditioner through it. Our dinners sat untouched in the bag on her table. Nobody was hungry.

"Any time now," I said, feeling angry.

"It's a good habit to put moisture back into the hair every two months or so," she told me in an automatic voice, like she was talking to a new client who didn't already know this. "Just another few minutes, and your hair will shine like the ocean on a sunny day."

"My hair is shiny enough," I told her.

She led me to the washing sink and unwrapped the towels.

After she rinsed out the conditioner and sat me in her chair, in front of the mermaid and the mirror, I knew the time had come for her to tell me. I knew it by the way she'd worked the conditioner through my ends so hard. And how her face seemed a million miles away, like she was thinking about something she'd never thought about before.

"Mama," I said finally, "I need to know." I watched her through strands of my wet hair, which were now combed straight out over my eyes and dripping little drops of creamy soft water from all that deep conditioning.

Mama nodded and I could see her give in. Her shoulders curled inward, and her face softened. She combed my hair from the back and the sides, walking barefoot around me with her professional scissors tucked into the front pocket of her working apron. I waited while she kept parting my hair and then combing it out, and parting it again in a different place. She looked tired. And a little sad.

Finally she took a deep breath. "It was in the middle of the winter," she said as she adjusted the black cape around my neck. "When the El Niño storms came and the weather station had to issue a flash flood warning for the whole county. Remember?"

"Yes."

"We had four inches of rain falling every hour for three days straight, and some of the houses on the hill above the harbor were beginning to show signs of slipping down with the mud." She concentrated on cutting a straight line of bangs.

"Are we almost done with the cutting, Mama?"

"Almost," she answered.

"Is this the part about Daddy?"

"I'm getting to it," she said. "There were little rivers of water running through the streets, and people were piling up sandbags around their homes. The palm trees were bent over sideways from the wind coming onshore so strong."

Mama went on with her story while the memory of that time swirled through my head. With the help of Luis and Frankie, we'd filled twenty-two burlap bags with beach sand and stacked them up against the doors of our house to keep the water from coming in. Our garage had leaked so much that there had been a puddle of water four inches deep standing around the fishing poles and crab nets that Daddy kept piled in the corner.

Luis had even closed the Swallow for a week straight, on account of the rain coming through the roof in places where the red tiles were separated or broken. He said there were only so many buckets of water a customer could be expected to walk around before it became bad for business.

"With the oil spill offshore having slowed down the real estate market already, your father knew the flooding meant selling houses would be impossible for a long time. The damage would take months to repair because according to him, we only had one good construction company in town." Mama sighed.

She was cutting wisps of blond off the back of my hair now. I watched them fall to the floor.

"Couldn't he get another job?" I asked.

Mama didn't answer.

"He always did before."

"He came by to see me at work that day," she said finally. "I was busy, and I couldn't take the time to talk to him just then, with one client processing color and another waiting for a cut. I guess he left before I could take a break because when I went outside to find him, he was gone."

"Where did he go?"

"Down south, to Mexico," Mama answered. "To get out of the rain and think, and come up with a new plan and a new job. Only problem was, when he got to the Mexican border, the police wouldn't let anyone through. The authorities had closed the border to all cars and trucks on account of the heavy rain causing so many mud slides in the area."

"It was that bad?"

Mama nodded and stopped cutting for a moment, pulling both sides of my hair down to see that they were even.

When she was positive that my cut looked perfect, she said, "Your father sat inside that small building at the border, the one where all the people who are stopped have to wait while the immigration officials check their papers. He tried to wait until the mud was bulldozed away and they opened the roads again."

Then her voice changed. "You see, Groovy," she said, "this is where your father should have remembered what I taught him and checked his daily horoscope instead of the *Daily Racing Form* he said was sitting on the table there. He should have seen that *that* day was *no* day to take any chances. Everyone knows not to take chances when there's a new moon. But . . ." She stopped and turned to look out the window.

"But what?" I leaned forward a little.

"But being a Sagittarius, he couldn't help himself." Mama's voice was louder now.

She put her comb and scissors down with a bang on her counter, and the mermaid fell over on her face. Mama was all set to blow-dry my new cut. But she unplugged her hair dryer and wrapped the cord around the handle, like she forgot the steps to finishing a haircut.

I pushed my hair to the side again. My breath caught in my throat. "What did he do?" I asked, ever so quiet, almost not wanting to hear what she was telling me.

Mama's voice sounded even madder. "What he should have done was driven straight home and given you back what was yours. The money he secretly took from the bank. Because he was listed as one of your guardians, he had access to Eleanor Robinson's money, and he took it with him." She stopped for a moment then and shook her head back and forth, sighing real long and loud. Her hands were firm on her hips, and her lips were bunched up.

My mouth dropped open as I looked at Mama. I couldn't believe what she was saying.

"Instead," she said, "he went to the only place *he* knew to go with that kind of money."

"Where did he go?" I stood up from the chair and began to breathe real fast because this was *not* the story I thought it was going to be after all. The words *he took it with him* played over in my head, making me dizzy, and I held on to the wall.

"Baby," Mama said, "I'm sorry. I know you had plans for that money, how you want to be a real cook. That's why this is so hard to tell you. Why I've been delaying telling you. I've been trying to think up another plan. It's why I brought up the idea about selling the strawberries." She reached to touch my cheek; her hand was soft.

I looked away. I wanted her words to disappear. I wanted my daddy to come back and everything to be normal again.

Mama turned my chin toward hers. She waited. I could feel that she didn't want to say anything more by the way her eyes searched my face, looking for the right words, the ones that didn't exist.

Then she whispered, "You see, he went to a racetrack to see the horses run. And he lost all that money on a single bet."

JASMINE TEA WITH LIMES

Mama and I walked home slowly from the salon.

Me with wet hair, and Mama with a look on her face like a teacher has when she passes back a test you didn't do so well on.

And I could feel that with every step my stomach was tightening.

But it was not the same stomach feeling I had when Daddy was arrested, because my hands did not sweat. Instead, I felt sick.

"Baby," Mama said when we came to the top of the hill, "being your mother, I thought it was best to try to get that money back. So it would be there when you were ready to use it for cooking school. But when I found out he lost every cent on a bet, well, I'm sure you can imagine how angry I was. I gave him a chance to get that money back, but he didn't."

She stopped then, and her black bag fell to the ground as she raised her fists high toward the lone stars peering through the leftover fog in the dark sky. She cursed them for her fate first. Then for mine.

"Do you know the value of that kind of money?" Mama asked the sky, with her neck bent backward, looking up.

She waited.

I looked up. I knew she remembered the names of all those stars. And that it was good luck when one of them shone more brightly than another. Or if they lined up in certain formations.

But all I could see was the Little Dipper.

She turned in circles as she held her arms out to the sides, still watching the sky. Her pink-painted toenails glowed in the dark on top of the black pavement, and her yellow hair blew around her face from the breeze. She looked beautiful to me, twirling like a maple seed does when it falls from its branch on a windy day. And as I watched her, I knew I loved her for taking such good care of me, worrying about my future, all the matters of my heart that'd obviously transferred automatically when I wasn't watching, just like she said they would.

After a minute she stopped and turned to look at me. "I don't know how to explain what your father did. I'm sorry." She shook her head. "Let's go home." She took my hand in hers because it was almost like I didn't know the way just then.

We walked up to our white house and to Mama's roses. The moonlight caught their petals, like tiny night-lights showing the way home. The smell of Listerine rose from the dirt, mint and orange mixed together.

She put her arms around me as the shock of all the news sank in deep.

"I can't believe Daddy did that," I told her, feeling my face grow hot.

Mama stopped at the front door and looked me over. Then she guided me into her bedroom instead of my own, saying she wanted to keep an eye on me for the night.

"Put these on," she told me, helping me change into my pajamas.

She slid me into the middle of her bed, tucking the soft, light-blue blanket tight around the edges of my legs and feet, making me look like a mummy.

"I'll be right back with some hot jasmine tea and some limes and honey, baby," Mama said.

"Mama?" I asked.

She turned to look at me. "What, baby?"

"When Daddy was being taken away in the police car, when he got into the backseat, there was this flower growing out of the sidewalk right there where the car was parked." I stopped, feeling tears start in my eyes. I remembered the chrome bumper on the car, how it had shone in the sun.

How now I understood why Daddy hadn't been able to talk about anything just then. And how his explanation hadn't really explained anything. Well, no wonder; it had been about my future.

Mama waited.

"It was a dandelion," I told her. "It was poking out of the concrete beside the wheel of the police car. And when Daddy got into the car, he stepped on it, accidentally, probably." I wiped my eyes and breathed deep.

Mama walked to the bed and sat down next to me. "It will grow back, baby. Dandelions are strong."

"He didn't watch where he was going," I said. Tears rolled down my cheeks. "He ruined it, Mama. He didn't watch, and now it's ruined." And I started crying like there was no tomorrow. But it wasn't the dandelion that made me so sad. It was how I was like the dandelion, minding my own business, waiting to grow and be something. And he hadn't seen me waiting.

SALTINES AND
LIQUID TYLENOL

~⌐

Mama didn't know what to do with me after that. I could tell by how long it took her in the kitchen. I couldn't believe how she carried on. "You want some tea, baby?" "I could fix you a plate of saltines." "Here you go, liquid Tylenol."

I heard her banging pots and filling the teakettle with water. It took her four tries to get the stove lit. When she finally came back, she brought two cups of steaming tea. I watched her squeeze limes into the cups and stir them with her little finger. I wondered why she didn't know that with tea, most people used lemons.

"Careful," she said, handing one to me. "It's hot."

"Thanks, Mama." I held the cup in my hands and the lime scent rose up in little puffs, stinging my eyes from the hot air-and-tears mixture.

Mama fluffed the pillows until they were big with air, and we leaned against them.

After a long time of blowing on the tea to cool it, she said, "Groovy, I did what I had to. When I found out he didn't have a way to put that money back in the bank, I wanted him to pay for what he'd done. So I called a lawyer. It took some time, but then your father was on his way to the city jail. I'm sure he won't be able to post the bail. And if that's the case, the judge will have to keep him there until his hearing because he might try to leave again." She looked me straight in the eyes then to make sure I was listening. Her gaze caused my tears to start again, and I looked down at the blankets.

"You see, baby"—she kissed the top of my

head—"I thought he should have to live with the consequences of his actions. And when he goes before the judge, the judge will tell him how to make it right, and give him his sentence. He may have to stay in jail several weeks."

I nodded but didn't say anything. I was afraid that if I tried to answer, or even looked up, I would start to cry hard. So I stared at her light-blue blanket, memorizing the crisscross stitching and forcing my brain to follow the over-under pattern so I couldn't think about Daddy anymore.

"I'm sorry about all of this, baby," Mama said after a while. She waited a long time between her words, giving me a chance to talk if I wanted. But I didn't. She pushed my hair from my face and tucked it behind my ears.

I sat still and calm, letting her fingers pull me into a peaceful feeling with the soft strokes while the space between her words and me got bigger.

"You should try to sleep now," she said finally, and took my teacup, setting it on the table next to her bed.

I slid down into the blankets. I let them cover my head, blocking out the lamplight, the air from the ceiling fan, the picture of Daddy in my head getting into that police car and how Officer Miguel stopping him had not been a mistake after all.

Mama lay gently beside me. She adjusted her feet. One outside of the covers and one inside, the way she always slept.

And as we fell asleep together, late that night in Mama's bed, I carefully and ever so slowly stretched my feet across the sheets to touch Mama's inside foot. I wanted to feel the anger she had inside her toward Daddy. I hoped it would travel through her leg and into mine, all the way up to my heart. That way, I wouldn't have to feel the hurt from what my daddy had done.

COFFEE *CON LECHE*

Sunday morning I waited in bed while Mama got dressed. I pretended to be asleep.

"I've got a training class at the salon this morning. Texturizing hair," she said. "But I'll be home before lunch. You try to rest this morning." She kissed the top of my head, and a lone strand of my hair stuck to her lip gloss, lifting up as she pulled away.

"I know you're awake. Did you hear me? I want you to rest some." She pushed hair from my face. "I called Luis. I asked him to order a case of the large strawberries. In case you decide you want to start making your chocolate-covered strawberries."

I didn't feel like answering. I didn't feel like dipping strawberries in chocolate sauce. I held my breath, waiting for her to leave.

But I heard her open the newspaper instead. "Well," Mama said finally. "There's nothing in here that will be of assistance today. I'm surprised. Usually this author is more accurate with her horoscopes. I'm gonna have to call the newspaper and complain. There's people trying to plan their lives around here.

"Good-bye, baby," she told me.

The smell of burned toast drifted from the kitchen. Even with me setting the toaster for her, she blackened every piece of bread. I wondered where my cooking abilities came from. Not from her.

I sat up and called Frankie on the telephone.

"Can you come over?" I asked him. I could hear Luis in the background chopping something on the counter.

"I'm helping Luis this morning. We got a big order of tacos for a party tomorrow. Someone's birthday. You sound weird. What's wrong?"

"Is that Groovy?" I heard Luis ask Frankie. "Tell her to come in if she wants. I could use another pair of hands today. Tell her I'll pay her for her help."

"Luis says—"

"I heard him," I told Frankie. "I'll come there."

"See ya," he answered.

I hung up the phone and thought how people were still celebrating birthdays and ordering food platters, and how things went on at their own speed no matter what sort of terrible news just got told.

I told myself, *Don't think about cooking school.* But as soon as I thought it, wouldn't you know my mind would think up all sorts of things about cooking, just because I told it not to.

But the worst thing was thinking that Frankie

had been right all along about my daddy. I was wrong and he was right.

Frankie, Luis, and I sat at the back counter next to a plate of forty chicken–black bean–green onion tacos before the Swallow opened up for business. We ate cinnamon toast and drank coffee *con leche* with mostly *leche* and actually only a little coffee out of tall Styrofoam cups.

I told them everything.

Frankie listened with a look on his face that said, *See, I knew you couldn't trust your father.*

Luis let the party order wait. He kept refilling our drinks, even though they didn't need refilling, while saying things like, "I can't believe it," and "I never would've thought."

When I got to the end, he sat down right next to me. He looked me in the eyes. Then he said, "Groovy, I'm very sorry about your father."

I nodded.

"And I'm sorry about you not having that money for cooking school. You know it's still a long way off before you're old enough to go, but in the meantime, I'll tell you what. I can teach you everything I know about food. It's mostly Mexican dishes and all, but I've got at least twenty more secret recipes. Ones you don't even know about."

I smiled at Luis. I'm here to tell you he would've given me his shop if he thought it would help.

"Plus, I'd be proud to sell your chocolate-covered strawberries."

"Your mom called about it early this morning," Frankie said.

"When she ordered a whole case of strawberries, well, I naturally asked what they were for," Luis told me.

"You think people would buy them?" I looked at Luis, feeling slightly hopeful for the first time since the news about Daddy.

"Let's try it out," he said, smiling big.

A soft knocking on the glass door in front of the shop interrupted us. Because of the SORRY, WE'RE CLOSED sign being in the way, we couldn't make out who it was. So Luis walked over and unlocked the door.

Frankie checked his watch. "It's not opening time yet," he told me, and I wondered who it could be.

The smell of the sea drifted inside as a black-haired lady made her way toward us. She took miniature steps, like she wasn't sure she should really come in. She seemed familiar to me, but by the way she wouldn't look me in the eye, I decided I didn't know her.

Her long hair was held in place by two butterfly-shaped crystal barrettes. Her eyes were dark, like the asphalt on the fishing docks. And her face was perfectly round with a rich girl's forehead, the kind Mama always pointed out to me in magazines.

"*Buenos días,*" she said to Luis in perfect Spanish.

"Good morning," Luis answered, and looked back to Frankie.

A loud thud sounded next to Frankie's feet. It echoed through the store, through the sudden quiet, like a thunderclap from far away brimming on the horizon to tell you it's making its way.

I looked to see what it was. His coffee *con leche* was spilling out from the Styrofoam cup around the bottom of his tennis shoes, staining the white leather and his laces. He stared at the lady like he couldn't believe what he was seeing. He didn't seem to notice the mess on the floor, or care.

"I'm here to see Francisco," she told us, walking toward Frankie, spreading her arms wide. Tears came from her black eyes, spilling down her face so fast, she stumbled as she reached out to him.

And then I remembered who she was by the way she knew Frankie's real name, how her eyes recognized him. And by the look on Frankie's face. How he tightened and backed away quickly while Luis went on high alert like a mother polar bear protecting a cub.

She was Zoila Maria Venicio, Frankie's mama. The one who'd sent the letters he refused to read. The one who left with only a carry-on.

And she was standing in the Swallow, right in front of us.

CHOCOLATE ICE CREAM VERSUS VANILLA ICE CREAM

~

"Gosh," Luis said, sounding a little surprised and kind of weird at the same time. "We didn't know you were in town. Did you come by boat?"

I could tell he knew Zoila right away. And I remembered the story about how she had married his father after his own mother had passed away from being sick when he was younger. How he and Frankie had become stepbrothers overnight, meeting only after their parents' wedding ceremony. He said he never understood how Zoila had been able to talk his father into buying that big fishing boat, and then sail it all over the world when there was plenty of good fishing right here in our area.

"Yes and no," Zoila told him. She wiped her face. It was easy to see that she was real nervous. "The boat was too long to dock at the marina here, so we left it down south. I took a taxi here to find Francisco." She looked at Frankie, her eyes taking him in, top to bottom. Francisco who everyone called Frankie because *Francisco* never fit him. "Your father had to stay with the boat and do some repairs," she said.

"Sounds like him," said Luis. "That boat always meant more to him than—" He stopped suddenly and frowned.

Zoila looked down at the ground. She wiped her remaining tears with her forearm. Red lipstick smeared lightly across her brown skin. After a second she turned to me.

"It's good to see you again, Groovy," she said in a new sparkly voice.

"You too," I said. "You look different. I didn't recognize you at first."

She smiled. "It has been a while. Francisco," she said quietly, walking slowly toward Frankie this time, "I think we should have a talk, somewhere private."

"I don't think so," Frankie answered. But it didn't sound like him. "We're about to open up for business." He backed into his stool so quick that it crashed to the floor and rolled sideways into the puddle of coffee.

"I'll get it," I told him. But he didn't seem to hear me.

"Just a few minutes," his mama said, and came even closer to him so that he could almost reach right out and touch her to make sure she was real after all this time. "I've only got a couple of hours before we go out to sea again. Please. This is important." She waited, her fingers twisting the gold-chain strap on her purse.

"I guess you could use the apartment upstairs." Luis pointed to the stairs. "Groovy and I will cover the shop until you're done."

"Thank you." Zoila reached to touch his shoulder. But he stepped back just a little. Enough so she couldn't.

She looked at him like she was trying to understand something. Then she walked toward the stairs, checking behind her to make sure Frankie was coming.

"Go on," Luis finally said to Frankie.

Frankie's face stayed stiff.

"I mean, she did come a long way," Luis added, in a way someone might if they had ordered chocolate ice cream for dessert, and the restaurant only had vanilla left. The way they would say, "Oh, all right, I guess I'll have the vanilla."

Frankie looked hard at Luis. Then he turned toward the window. I knew he was trying not to remember her carry-on suitcase, or her promise to be right back. I knew he was trying not to look at her on purpose. I knew it by the way he held his hand against his stomach and kept it there, like he needed an orange Tums.

Finally he walked up the stairs, slowly, heavily. He looked like a person who just got sent to the principal's office for getting into trouble.

It seemed like they were up there for hours. Luis and I covered the shop, tending to the cash register, making change for customers who needed quarters for the parking meters, and selling his famous tacos.

But the whole time, our eyes were saying to each other, *I wonder what is happening up there.* Then we'd glance to the top of the stairs at the same time, waiting for the door to open.

FRANKIE'S FAVORITE
KIND OF SANDWICH

~~

Here's what happened next. (In list form because
things happened one after the other. Like dom-
inoes falling. But separate.)

1. The door slammed open and Frankie
   came down the stairs.
2. I dropped a roll of quarters from
   being startled. They scattered
   everywhere, rolling into corners
   and spinning in half circles before
   tipping over.

3. Frankie's mama rushed after him, trying to keep up in her high heels.
4. Frankie pushed the front door of the Swallow wide open.
5. The bells chimed extra loud, hitting the glass so hard I thought it might break.
6. I yelled to Frankie to stop.
7. He walked to the taxi parked in front of the shop and stopped.
8. Frankie's mama caught up to him.
9. Luis and I ran to the front window to look out.
10. The taxi driver started his car again, getting ready to leave.

But Frankie's mama didn't get inside the taxi. Instead, she held her arms open at her sides with her palms up. Like a person does when they are asking what else they could have done.

I could see how Frankie had grown to look like her. How he had the same straight black hair, the same nose, the same brown skin. Even the same hands. I could see how he might've been just like her in his ways, if he'd always lived with her. But she didn't even know his favorite kind of sandwich—grilled cheese on white—or that he'd been voted class vice president last year.

"He looks upset," I told Luis in a quiet voice.

"He's got a lot to be upset about."

"Maybe you should go out there," I said.

Luis looked out the window again.

"Well?" I waited for him to go help Frankie.

"They need to work this out themselves," he finally answered.

"But it looks like he really needs you."

"God knows what he needs better than I do," Luis said.

I walked to the glass door, thinking I would go out there myself, and pushed it open, but something made me stop. Maybe it was the way Frankie looked like he was going to cry if I came too close, or the way his mama sighed so loud just then; I could tell she was running out of things to say.

I backed into the shop, letting the weight of the door push me inside again. My hands gripped the silver bar as I watched them through the glass.

After a while, I saw her take a white envelope out of her purse. She tried to give it to Frankie. But he wouldn't take it.

"What do you think it is?" I asked Luis.

"I don't know. Maybe some more letters or money. But I'm only guessing."

"Maybe some pictures," I told him, and imagined it was a collection of photographs from all the places they'd been while sailing the world catching fish.

His mama begged him to take it, holding it between their bodies. Like a tiny drop of glue she hoped would keep them connected.

She kept talking to him, and when it seemed she finally knew that what she was saying would make no difference, she put the envelope back into her purse, stepped close to Frankie, and hugged him. And he let her. But he didn't put his arms around her. Instead, his arms lay flat at his sides.

She hugged him real hard.

And by the way she held so tight to him, it looked to me like she was very sorry.

But then Frankie moved away from her. He started back toward the shop.

"What's he doing?" I asked Luis. I felt a panic inside.

Luis shook his head. "This is just like Frankie. I've been telling him that she would come back someday. I said, 'She won't have you staying with me forever, you know.'" He sighed, and I could picture the two of them standing together on the jetty, Luis talking, telling him about his mother. Frankie, not wanting to care if she ever came back.

His mama leaned against the taxi like it was the only thing holding her up, like her legs had stopped working. Tears ran down from her black-asphalt eyes.

And that's when my stomach went tight, and my breath stopped, and a very bad feeling came over me. Because it was plain to see that he had made up his mind.

I watched Frankie walk away from his mama that morning. And with each step he took, I knew he was carving a deeper hole into his heart.

THE PART OF
MARISOL THAT SHINES

I've got another recipe for you, Groovy, became
Luis's favorite seven words. Every time I stopped
in the Swallow on my way home from school, he
was handing me a piece of paper with a different
secret passed down from his Aunt Regina. Fried
ice cream, tortilla soup, stuffed green chilies; you
name it.

Don't get me wrong, I was thankful to have
the recipes, and I taped each one carefully into my
cooking notebook and all, but I was pretty sure it
wasn't anything like formal training.

There was nothing in Luis's recipes about the things I wanted to know, like the exact proper amount of time to cool a cake straight from the oven before thinking of frosting it.

Even Ms. Dixon-Green, our school librarian, couldn't find the answer.

"I'll look into ordering a cooking reference book," she told me. "But it could take a while."

Every day at lunch recess, I'd wander into the library and make my way to her desk. "You found out anything yet?" I'd ask her, like my very life suddenly depended on knowing the correct number of minutes to cool a cake.

She never did.

One day she handed me an empty cake-mix box. "It's about ten minutes before removing the cake from the pan, and then it says to cool *completely* before frosting," she said. "According to Betty Crocker, at least." She pointed to the directions listed on the back of the box.

"I *know* what the box says," I told her, as if *I* hadn't already memorized what Betty Crocker's instructions were for cake baking. "But the *skin* of the cake is tender for a long time. I wish they'd tell us how long *completely* cool is."

Ms. Dixon-Green sighed and looked again at the directions. "That's true," she said. "I hate it when the frosting pulls up little bits of the cake."

I stopped going to the library at lunchtime after that.

I decided maybe it was more of a heat-and-cooling scientific thing, and made plans to ask Miss Johnson instead.

When the case of strawberries came in to the Swallow from the fruit market, Luis delivered them to my house himself.

"Can't wait to try one," he said. Which is exactly the kind of thing Luis would say.

"Thanks. I'll bring them over when I'm done," I said.

It took me most of the afternoon to finish the first batch. Mama kept calling home from the salon. "How's it coming?" "Do you have enough chocolate?" "Don't burn yourself on the stove, please." I stopped answering the phone.

The whole time I was working, I kept thinking about how years from now, when I'd finally saved up enough money for cooking school, I would write in the front of my cookbook, where the dedication usually is, how hard work had dominated every second of my life, day after day, dipping strawberries into two parts dark chocolate and one part milk chocolate. Lining tray after tray of strawberries. And not just any strawberry, but the extra-big ones that take at least four bites to eat. The kind where the chocolate crumbles off after the first bite, making you catch it with your free hand and pop it in your mouth before it melts. The good kind.

When I got through most of the case, it was almost dinnertime. I watched the sun from our kitchen window as it lowered toward the line where the red-orange sky met the blue-green ocean while I ate three of my strawberries to hold me over until dinner. Then I covered the tray with tinfoil, pressing the edges of the foil carefully around the sides so as not to crush anything.

You should have seen how slowly I walked to the Swallow. I'm here to tell you that turtles could've passed me.

As I neared the shop, I saw Marisol hunched over the sidewalk in front. She was drawing an enormous flock of birds flying in the sky. Felix was sitting on the yellow bench, his feet swinging wildly back and forth, eating a purple Popsicle.

"Marisol's sketching the return of the swallows today. We've been here since we got out of school," he told me.

She stood up, wiping chalk on her shorts. "Luis said it would be nice since this is the area they come to and all." She walked up good and close to me, looking at my tinfoil-covered tray. "What's that?"

"Nothing," I told her.

Felix hopped off the bench and walked over. He lifted a corner of the foil back and peeked inside. "They're strawberries," he said. "With chocolate on them."

I looked at Marisol, feeling annoyed that she knew.

"What type of food are they?" Felix asked. His Popsicle was melting down his wrist, a thin line of purple tattooing his skin.

"They're a dessert," I said.

"No, I mean what *type* of food are they? Like where would you put them in the phone book? My dad's restaurant is under *Mexican Food*," he told me.

"They're a dessert," I said again. "They don't have a category." I made my way around him toward the front door of the shop, avoiding Marisol's sketch the best I could.

"You gonna sell those?" Marisol asked.

"Maybe." I reached to open the door, balancing my tray with one hand.

"You ever sold any before?" she asked.

"Marisol sold one of her sketches in the restaurant yesterday. To a man with a good eye for art," Felix said. "She gets to keep all the money."

I stopped. My hand gripped the door handle.

"Really?" I asked her. "Someone bought one of your pictures? For real?"

She shrugged like it was no big deal, but her eyes said it was. "Yeah. I told you, people enjoy my art. I'm gonna be in galleries soon."

I stood holding my tray, watching her, the happiness floating off her. The look on her face that said, *I knew this would happen all along.*

A breeze rushed in, sending her hair across her face, making her blink. But I could still see it, the part of her that shone that I wanted to be too.

Standing there, I suddenly needed to tell someone my dream. Someone who drew pictures of birds on sidewalks because she loved to. Someone who wanted to be in galleries and sold her sketches to strangers. Someone who believed in almost impossible things happening.

I walked over to Marisol and slowly, carefully, lifted the tinfoil off my tray of strawberries. Felix stepped up, putting his face against the edge of the tray, his eyes as big as oranges.

"Those are nice," he said.

"You see," I said to Marisol, "I want to go to professional cooking school. I have since third grade. I'm hoping to sell these to save money so I can go when I'm older. I don't know how else to get there. I had a savings account, but it's gone now," I heard myself say, and everything was quiet. Right away, I wished I hadn't told her so much.

Marisol looked straight at me. I could tell she was thinking about what I'd said by the way she squinted and tipped her head.

I was just about to put the tinfoil back over my tray and go inside the Swallow, when she opened her mouth to talk.

She didn't say *It'll never work* or *You should think up another plan*. She didn't even roll her eyes, or tell me, *Good luck*.

She said, "How much are they then?" And she reached into her pocket and handed over all the money she had.

THE (BIG) CARDBOARD
BOX IN THE HALL CLOSET

Reports from Luis were good. He sent word with Frankie, who stopped me outside my locker at school the next day.

"They all sold," he said. "And Luis thinks you should bring in another batch."

The happiness of hearing this news distracted me so much that, in class, it caused me to accidentally do the odd-numbered math problems instead of the evens that Miss Johnson had assigned.

When I got home that day, Mama called the wholesale fruit market in the next town, said we needed to lower our costs, that the test had gone well, and I was in business for real now.

I knew I'd be able to earn enough money to do whatever I wanted. I knew this deep inside because Marisol—yes, *Marisol*—had believed it too.

I'd see her at the Swallow most days after school buying two chocolate-covered strawberries—one for her and one for Felix.

"I'm contributing to your cause," she'd say, for which I'd always thank her.

"I understand about wanting something," she'd say.

And I'd tell her, "I know you do." And a feeling would settle over me like we were the same at our very inner core, and that each strawberry she bought connected us together even more.

I put aside my usual dinner-menu planning and cooking for me and Mama. I concentrated only on chocolate-covered strawberries. I wore a path in the cement from my house to the Swallow with all the delivering. Mama kept my earnings safe in a new account at the bank. One that had only one name on it: mine.

At night, after I'd done my homework, we'd sit in lawn chairs on the back patio and dream about me being Groovy Robinson, Fortune 500 company owner.

Next to all this, though, I still thought a lot about Daddy. I thought about him during music class when Mr. Perez asked the class to play a slow song. I'd play that song on my oboe like I was the one who'd wrote it, like every high and low note was telling my story.

Thoughts about Daddy would sneak into my head even when there was nothing to remind me of him. Tying my shoes. Riding the bus. During math when Miss Johnson explained prime factorization with variables. A lot came to me during math.

In my mind, there were certain things I wondered about. Plus, I'd been mulling over the thought of getting into Great-grandmother Eleanor Robinson's pages and pages of stories.

The ones she'd left to me and told Mama I'd know what to do with. So far, though, no ideas were coming to me.

"Frankie?" I said to him the next Saturday morning as me, Marisol, and Felix sat at the back counter of the Swallow watching Luis make flour tortillas from scratch. "Can you help me with something?" A fresh tray of my strawberries sat next to the cash register. Two were already gone, bought by you-know-who.

"What?" he asked. He'd been going around not bothering to smile much or tell anyone about his mama, acting like nothing had happened the week before. Like she'd never appeared out of the blue looking for him. But I knew he was thinking about her. I knew by the way he held his stomach, his arm wrapped tight around his waist, holding everything in, how he tried to act all ho-hum.

"It's a cardboard box," I answered, and then added, "a big one."

"Does it have chalk inside?" asked Felix.

"No," I said, and Marisol rolled her eyes.

Luis looked confused. "Where's this box?" He dusted his rolling pin and the countertop in flour. Tiny white particles floated in the air around his hands as he rolled out the circles of dough.

"In our hall closet at home," I told everyone. "It's been there a really long time. It's marked *ER*, for *Eleanor Robinson*, in black marker. Mama told me it was mine." I traced the initials *ER* in the flour on the countertop with my finger.

Marisol's eyes lit up, and she immediately began drawing a swallow in the flour.

Felix watched and then started to write his name.

"What's inside?" Frankie asked.

"Stories," I told them. "They're written by my great-grandmother. She left them to me. I guess there could be other stuff, too. I'm hoping there's something there that might help me. I mean, since it was her money in the first place."

Marisol glanced at me, looking confused.

"My savings account. The one I told you about that's gone now," I said.

"Right." She nodded that she remembered and then continued drawing a pair of wings in flight.

"Marisol, how do you make an *X* again?" Felix asked. He'd made several *H*s next to the *I* in his name. It was easy to see he was still learning his letters.

Marisol sighed loudly, like it might actually kill her to stop her drawing. "Like this," she said, scratching a large *X* next to his *H*s. "It's only two lines, crisscrossed—like a bird claw, but simpler. Remember?"

"Oh, yeah," he said, smiling.

She sighed even louder.

"Well," Luis said, "you sure are a good printer, Felix."

He beamed, then frowned. "I'll never be an artist, though. Marisol was an artist by the time she was three."

We all looked at her. She was working on the bird's tail, its feathers fanned out perfectly. She worked so hard, without looking up, that I wondered if she heard us.

Finally Luis said, "Felix, I know you'll be something good someday. Maybe a business owner like your dad."

Felix smiled again. "Probably I'll be that."

Luis put down his rolling pin and wiped his hands, while Frankie pressed his palms against his stomach and looked out the window. I could tell Frankie was deciding something big.

"Let's check out that box," Frankie told me finally, like he was relieved to have something to think about other than his stomachaches.

I smiled at him.

"Can I come too?" Felix asked.

"We have to go home now," Marisol told him, and she jumped off her stool and held her hand out for Felix. I could tell by the way she waited for her brother with her hand held out firm that she loved him. Even if she did roll her eyes and sigh sometimes when he talked.

"This was a good medium to work with," Marisol told Luis, pointing to the flour. "Thanks for the experience. It's given me some new ideas."

Then she turned to me. "See ya later," she said.

"Okay," I answered.

"Glad to be of help," Luis said.

Marisol and Felix walked toward the front of the shop.

"I wish I could see what's in that box," Felix called over his shoulder to us as Marisol dragged him out the door.

Frankie helped Luis clean the flour off the counter. Then we made our way to the box shoved behind Mama's old hair dryers in the closet. So I could see for myself about the original Eleanor Robinson.

BURNED TUNA MELTS

"You could've done it yourself. It's not that heavy." Frankie stepped back and stretched his arms up. We'd slid the box into the middle of the kitchen floor. The smell of burned tuna melts and lemon-scented dish soap hung in the air. Mama, who'd taken over the routine cooking, had made sandwiches while home from the salon on her lunch break. She left them on a paper plate for me with a note saying, "*Bon appétit.* According to your horoscope today, good things are in store."

The frying pan lay in the sink unwashed.

Drops of water splashed in threes from the faucet. *Drip, drip, drip. Drip, drip, drip.* Something Daddy had never got to fixing.

"I thought the box would be heavy because it's so big," I told him. "Let's open it."

It took us a few tries with the scissors to cut it open. Masking tape and years of heat waves had glued the seams shut, protecting what was inside.

When we finally peeled it away, the odor of dust and old paper came into the room, circling around us.

"What's this?" Frankie grabbed a yellowish crumpled piece of paper the size of a dollar bill. It was very wrinkled but looked like someone had tried their hardest to smooth it out. Like maybe they'd almost thrown it away but then thought, *No, this belongs in here after all.*

"It looks like an article about her life," I told him, thinking that it was probably the closest I would ever come to knowing her.

Frankie looked it over. "It says that she lived

in New York, that she had one daughter, a grand-daughter, and a great-granddaughter. . . . That's you." He looked up. "It also says she wrote a lot of books." He stopped and gave the article to me.

I looked at the picture of her. She was not smiling, but she looked real smart, and I wondered if I would look like that someday when I was older.

I put the article on the kitchen table and we unpacked the rest of the box. An envelope fell to the ground next to my legs. In perfect cursive handwriting, it read, "To: Eleanor Robinson." For a second I thought it must have been for her, but then I realized it was for me.

"Open it," Frankie said. "It's addressed to you."

"I know," I answered, thinking how Frankie always got things before I did. Inside was a letter written in the same handwriting. "It must be from her." My heart pounded.

"Well, what does it say?"

I stood up. I held the letter with both hands, like the words might have been written by a past president. "I'll read it to you."

To my dearest great-granddaughter,
Eleanor Robinson,
I leave to you all of my belongings,
everything that meant something to
me. I regret not having known you,
but I'm certain I would have loved
you.

From your great-grandmother,
Eleanor Robinson

"She sounds nice," Frankie said after a minute. He picked up the newspaper article and looked at her picture again. "She doesn't look nice, but she sounds nice."

The words *I'm certain I would have loved you* rang in my head. "She *was* nice," I told him. "I think we should look at the stories. There might be something in there, like a message or a clue."

"You mean about your father and what happened?"

"Maybe."

"I doubt it." He reached into the box and took

out a very old book written by Isaac Asimov. Its pages were slightly yellow and some were torn. "She wasn't a fortune-teller."

I took the book from him and held it. The cover showed a picture of what looked like a swirling galaxy and rows of spaceships flying around. I'd never seen anything so special. And I felt an overwhelming love for my great-grandmother, who had once read to my mama from these very pages. "Frankie, don't be so negative," I told him.

He shrugged.

"I know you're mad. Do you wanna tell me what your mama said to you last week?"

"No," he told the kitchen floor.

I waited.

The kitchen faucet dripped.

Finally he stood up and took a fresh roll of Tums from his pocket, opening it with his fingernail. Cherry, lemon, lemon, orange. He ate the fourth one. Then he reached into the box and took out the rest of the papers, a stack at least eighteen inches high, and set them on the table. "I guess we could look through them," he said.

It took some time, but we figured out there were three stories there, with a summary for each one.

I read the first summary. "It's about a deadly virus that creeps up through a cavern in the desert," I told Frankie. "And aliens come down from space to heal the human race."

"That doesn't sound like it would help with your situation." He grinned his I-told-you-so grin and picked up the next one.

I sighed, thinking how science fiction was not at all like real life. Maybe he was right.

"Here's one where a boy travels though time to the future and discovers a colony of people on Mars who are the only living species left from Earth." Frankie held up the summary of the second story. "I'd like to read this one."

"Maybe later. This is *serious*, Frankie."

"Sorry." He put the story down and picked up the last one. I watched him skim the summary page.

"What's it about?"

"Looks like another undiscovered colony of people. Only this one is living on a space station, orbiting Earth. She sounds like a good writer, though. These would make good books."

"I guess so." I didn't care just then if she'd written award-winning books.

Frankie walked to the kitchen sink and put his hands under the faucet, catching the drips in his palms. "I wish there would've been something in there that you wanted." He looked out the window, the same way he'd been staring at the ocean lately. Finally he said, "Oh, well. Just forget about it."

"How can you put things out of your head like that, and pretend like your mama didn't come?"

Frankie shrugged.

"I mean, I can't just *not* think about things that happen. Like yesterday on my way to catch the school bus, I said to myself, 'Okay, I'll take the long way to the bus stop. The way along the shore. And I'll pick up just one seashell—one.'"

I held up one finger. "'If a hermit crab pokes his legs out, I'll go see my daddy in jail. I'll ask him why he did it. I'll find out what happened—from his side.' Frankie, I must have picked up fourteen seashells before I found one with a hermit crab living inside. It was like I *wanted* to find one."

Frankie stared at me like I was speaking Latin.

"Don't you get it? I want to know *his* side." Feeling exhausted from everything, I leaned my head against the box, and it slid backward. As I pulled it back, I saw an envelope lying on the bottom, tucked into the corner. Something Frankie had missed when he'd unpacked the stories. It read, HARBOR BANK, 12 HARBOR DRIVE.

I climbed to my knees, grabbed it, and tore it open. "It's a key!" I showed it to Frankie. It was silver and shiny, and just bigger than a quarter. I held it up to the light coming through the window. Its reflection darted around the kitchen walls as I turned it over and over.

Frankie walked closer. "Hold on," he said.

"It has the number one hundred seventy-three engraved on it."

It was true. On the back were three small numbers that could be seen if we looked close enough. And I remembered seeing one just like it last summer when Daddy had taken me with him to the safe-deposit boxes inside the bank where he kept his insurance policies and coin collections. He said he had to keep them there so they'd never get lost, and those boxes were the one place in the world where things would be completely protected. Even from fire.

"It's for the safe-deposit boxes at the bank," I told Frankie.

"Really?" His eyes came back to life.

"I think so."

The doorbell rang three times suddenly, like whoever was out there ringing it was having some kind of actual emergency.

I ran to open the door. Marisol stood holding Felix's hand. He grinned up at me.

"He won't stop talking about your mystery

box," said Marisol. "I finally had to bring him up." She rolled her eyes.

"I told her there could be treasure inside," Felix said.

Marisol rolled her eyes again.

Frankie came to the door. "We didn't find any treasure, but we found this key." He held it up to show them.

"See?" Felix said to Marisol. "A key to *open* the treasure."

"Actually, I'm pretty sure it opens one of the safe-deposit boxes at the bank," I told them. "I was just on my way over there."

"That's where treasure is usually kept," Felix said, like he'd seen some just yesterday in a safe-deposit box. "It's not kept buried anymore."

I didn't want to tell him that treasure didn't really exist these days, but Marisol didn't have a problem with it.

"I told you, there's no such thing as finding treasure. That's only in books. And movies."

Felix pouted. "Are you sure?"

I bent down to him. "If I find anything good, I'll let you know," I told him.

"Thanks," Marisol said. And by the way she said it, I could tell she really was thankful, and that there was a little part of her that looked like she hoped I might find something, just so Felix could see it.

"I'll walk into town with you," I told Marisol and Felix.

"Can I hold the key?" asked Felix.

I nodded and gave it to him. Then I quickly packed all of Great-grandmother's stories back into the brown box and pushed it into the closet.

The three of us headed for the bank while Frankie started back to the shop to meet Luis.

I was sure the answer I was looking for would be inside box number 173.

FANCY SIGNATURE WITH LOOPS ON THE *E* AND THE *R*

Here's the good thing about living in a small town: You get to know most everyone. Here's the bad thing about living in a small town: You get to know most everyone.

So when we peeked through the window at the bank, I was relieved to see that I had definitely not met the man who was sitting behind the desk where the safe-deposit boxes were. Because I was in no mood to explain to anyone who knew me why I wasn't with my mama, or my daddy, visiting the bank.

Marisol and Felix waved good-bye and started across the street toward their father's restaurant. I heard Felix talking the whole way. "Do you think she'll find gold? Do you think pirates put it there? Do all pirates know about banks?"

Marisol didn't answer.

I stood on the corner of the pink stucco bank building, gathering my courage and making a plan to get into that box. The sun beat down hard in yellow blurs, spreading mirage waves along the sidewalk and reflecting from the huge bank windows onto my face.

I thought about Daddy and how we'd been here together last summer. We'd come after a Saturday morning at the dog races because he'd needed to put some things away so they'd be safe. I remembered how he'd told me over and over, "Groovy, a safe-deposit box is the best place for important things."

That's when it came to me. *What if Daddy had secretly put all of Great-grandmother's money in the safe-deposit box? What if Mama'd been wrong all along? After all, she probably didn't even know about Daddy keeping important things there.*

I felt overwhelmed with relief. That had to be it. Daddy hadn't really *lost* all that money on a bet. He'd put it in the safest place possible. People all over the world were probably doing the same exact thing this very minute.

Feeling this sudden happiness, I noticed the sky's perfect blue color, the way the birds on the electrical wire above me were singing so perfect. The way the smell of seaweed and salt floated even more perfectly through the warm air.

I smiled and walked inside the bank. I imagined saying to anyone who stopped me, *Oh yes, I'm here to get into my safe-deposit box again, like I was last week. I get into it all the time. You might have seen me before because of all the times I am here.* I made my way to the safe-deposit box area, like a person does when they bring the lunch count and roll call up to the school office for their teacher. With authority.

And slightly on a mission.

"Hello, Groovy." Pastor Ken suddenly stood in front of me, holding a large envelope marked PETTY CASH. "How are you today?" He smiled his usual big smile.

I looked around quickly to see if anyone else I knew was inside that I hadn't seen through the window. "Fine," I told him.

He smiled again. Then he said, "How are you and your mother getting along since . . . well, since your father's been gone?" He stepped closer to me. "Luis mentioned what happened."

"We're fine," I said. I thought about how Daddy would be getting out of jail as soon as I showed Mama the money that'd been inside the safe-deposit box all along.

"Why don't you bring your mother with you to church when I get back in a few weeks? I'm leaving next week for our annual mission trip to Mexico with all this money we've been collecting. Our best year yet for donations." He held out the envelope.

"I'll try," I said, knowing what Mama would say about that.

He smiled even bigger then. "You might want to think about coming with us for a week next year when you're older. We go over spring break. Luis is considering coming with Frankie next year. There's always a lot to be done, painting, cleaning. You could even help with the food like you help Luis at the Swallow."

"Maybe I could," I said in my most polite voice that meant I would think about it but that Mama would probably say no.

He nodded. "I'll see you when I get back then."

"Okay," I told him. I watched Pastor Ken stroll out the door and down the street. When I was certain he was far enough away, I walked toward the man sitting behind the desk.

"May I help you, young lady?" he asked me. He had a reddish face with some sweat on his forehead, and wore a blue suit and tie with a gold name tag pinned on his left pocket, which read, MR. HUGHES. And he was looking at me through glasses that made his eyes look twice as big as normal. Being the kind of important man he was, Mr. Hughes had papers and files all over his desk.

"I need to get into box number one hundred seventy-three, please," I said. "It's important."

"Hmmm," said Mr. Hughes, and he looked me over.

"I have a key," I replied, extra nice, and reached into my pocket, pulling it out to show him it was true.

Mr. Hughes's nose scrunched up as he looked at the key, leaning forward just a little. He pushed his glasses back into place.

"That does indeed appear to be one of our safe-deposit box keys," he said finally.

I let out a sigh of relief that traveled through the air between us, lifting up the front strands of his hair just a little.

He frowned and matted his hair back down with his hand. It stuck to the beads of sweat that he smeared across his forehead.

"What did you say your name was? We'll need you to sign the signature card before you can get into the box," Mr. Hughes explained.

I followed him to the table by the file cabinet. He walked extra slow. Like the heat was making him do things at half speed. Then he pulled open a large drawer that had hundreds of white cards in it, like the old card catalog drawers at the library that tell which shelf each book can be found on.

"Eleanor Robinson," I told him. "Would you like to see my ID? I have one from school with my picture on it." I handed him my key. I thought, *Don't tell him too much. The secret to lying is to not tell too much.* But I couldn't stop. "Yeah, my mama sent me down here to check on some papers. She wants me to make sure they're still safe."

"Miss Robinson," he said, "you keep the key to open your box, and I will get the matching key to assist you. And you may show me your picture then."

"Oh," I answered, feeling embarrassed. "See, well, we've got some important information I need to take a look at in there. It's about, well, it's about something very important."

He thumbed through the white cards.

"My mama has one-fourth ownership in the beauty salon up the street—you may have heard of it, the Secret Styling Hair and Nail Salon—and she wants me to verify her name and vital information on those papers."

"Hmmm," Mr. Hughes said.

"She would come herself, but she's pretty booked up and all. Saturdays are her busiest day. She's actually done a movie star just recently. So you can imagine her schedule."

Mr. Hughes leaned closer to the cards, squinting through his glasses.

I started to worry that it wouldn't be under my name after all. My foot tapped the floor. *Please be there. Please be there.*

"Ahh . . . here we are, Miss Robinson, your signature card. Your name does appear to be on the account," he said *finally*, and placed it on the table. He handed me a pen and pointed to where I should sign.

"Thank you." I smiled to be polite.

I looked at the card. There were two signatures on it. The first was the same that had been on the letter written to me from Great-grandmother. I knew right away it was her writing. And I realized then that my signature and the one on the card, written by the original Eleanor Robinson, had to match. Otherwise Mr. Hughes was not going to let me into that box. I knew this from going with Daddy last summer to see his coins.

The second signature was Daddy's. He'd signed his name in black ink under Great-grandmother's.

I leaned over the card, carefully studying my great-grandmother's writing. It was much fancier than my own writing. I worried that I could not make my handwriting match hers. So I lifted the pen over her signature to get a feel for it, to trace it in the air, but Mr. Hughes cleared his throat real loud to hurry me along.

"Sorry," I told him.

Then I just signed my name, in the fanciest way I could, with loops on the *E* and the *R*, and a big curve up at the end that curled around into a half circle. Kind of like the swirls in peppermint candy. "There!" I said, and put the pen down on that table with a bang.

Mr. Hughes picked up the card and looked at it up close.

"Is it okay?"

He held it to the window, letting the light fall onto my handwriting.

I'm here to tell you that I could barely breathe while I waited for him to make up his mind.

"It appears to be in order," Mr. Hughes finally answered. "Let me show you to the safe-deposit boxes."

Well, I knew my signature wasn't anything like Great-grandmother's, with hers having the self-confidence that comes from being a famous writer for many years, and mine being from just a girl in sixth grade. So I was thankful that Mr. Hughes must not have been able to see real good, even with his glasses.

I followed him into the small room.

"Here we are, Miss Robinson," Mr. Hughes said. "The safe-deposit box room."

"Thanks," I told him, looking around. There were rows of boxes along all four walls, in three sizes: small, medium, and large. In the middle of the room there was a table with a chair. I found Daddy's box on the back wall, number 1199, the smallest size.

Mr. Hughes showed me to my box then, which turned out to be the medium size. We put our keys in the locks at the same time. Then he told me to turn my key to the left while he lifted the box out from the wall, setting it on the table.

I put my hands on top of it and sat down in the chair, smiling. I'd been so caught up in everything that I'd forgotten about important things needing to go into a safe-deposit box. I pictured myself telling Mama how it had all been a big misunderstanding.

"Take your time, young lady," Mr. Hughes told me as he walked out of the room. "We don't close until four P.M."

NOTHING

Here's what was in the box: nothing. Well, nothing good at least. There wasn't any money—not even *one* dollar bill. Instead, I found seven lottery tickets, each with all the numbers crossed out, a newspaper showing more numbers circled in red pen, and a bank book that had $25,000.00 subtracted to only one number: zero.

I stared at that bank book.

I breathed in deep.

I stood up from the chair.

I sat back down again.

I studied the lottery tickets.

I read over the newspaper.

I wiped my hands on my shorts.

I knew Daddy's side now, without even talking to him.

I thought and thought about him. All I knew about him, and my feelings for him. And suddenly, everything that was in that box came falling down all around like a cold February storm onto my memory of who he was. Mama had been right. He'd taken the money and gambled it away. The evidence was right in front of me.

"How come you did this?" I asked him, knowing he couldn't hear me.

The feelings started real slow, like tiny raindrops that can't make up their minds if they're going to pour from the clouds, or pass through with the breeze.

But then the more I looked at his handwriting in the bank book—the zero scratched in black pen—the faster those drops fell, until it felt like I was sitting in a big, blowing thunderstorm. And just like those storms that can be so sneaky, I didn't see it coming. And before I knew it, I felt soaking wet, with nowhere to go.

So I sat there for a long time, until I shivered from all the cold swirling around me.

And then it happened. It started coming up into my toes, staying there for a minute, waiting to see if I would push it away.

But I didn't.

So it crept up past my knees, and then into my stomach, finally finding its way to my heart. Where it stopped and settled in deep.

And here's what I thought: I wished I'd never found what was in that box because feeling mad at Daddy was a million times worse than feeling sad.

EL NIÑO

I must've been in that room for a long time. I couldn't say for sure because there's no way to track time while trying to understand something completely different about a person you thought was someone else. Especially after years of me saying to people, *Oh no, my daddy's not like that. My daddy's this, or my daddy's that.*

I'd gone around my whole life believing what he'd told me, like what he'd said was just how things were. Mama had said he'd taken the money, that he'd lost it on a bet, but it wasn't until I saw his handwriting in the bank book that it seemed real to me. It wasn't until I saw for myself all his *different* ways of trying to win money that I knew how much he'd been lying to me and Mama.

So when Mr. Hughes knocked on the door and stuck his head in the room, I couldn't believe what he was saying.

"Only twenty minutes until closing, Miss Robinson." He tapped his watch.

"Okay," I answered. I knew he was going to make sure I followed the rules, so I started to pack up everything real fast.

He waited for me outside the door so he could lock up the room. "Is everything in order?" he asked.

"Sort of," I answered. But I didn't think I should tell him about the stolen money, being that he was in the bank business and all. So I started to walk toward the front door, pushing my key deep into my pocket.

I knew I needed to get out of that bank fast because the climate in there was even worse than the middle of an El Niño storm.

NOT SLOPPY JOES WITH SWEET ONIONS

I decided to tell everyone to please call me Eleanor from then on. *Groovy* didn't fit anymore. I said, "Mama, could you please start calling me Eleanor? I'm too old to be called Groovy. I have decided I look more like an actual Eleanor and not a Groovy." That kind of thing.

But the truth was, because it was the nickname Daddy had given me, I didn't want it. I didn't exactly tell her that part, though.

Late that afternoon, I put the safe-deposit key back into the brown box in the closet. I pushed it way down deep, past all those science fiction stories and the Isaac Asimov book.

Mama mysteriously took to keeping secrets too. When she brought in the mail, I saw her stuff a certain letter into her pocket as she flipped through the pile.

"What's that?" I finally asked.

"What?" she said.

"That envelope you put in your pocket."

"Nothing," she said, smiling all fake, like I was back in kindergarten and couldn't tell the difference between her real smiles and her forced ones.

"Nothing, as in nothing? Or nothing, as in you don't wanna show me?" I said.

She turned her back to me and immediately started straightening up things around the sink. Yellow dish soap. Rubber gloves. Partially used Brillo pads.

The way she got so busy with things that didn't matter, I figured the letter must have something to do with Daddy.

I decided I wouldn't tell Mama I'd been to the bank after that. Even though I'm pretty sure this was the kind of thing she'd want to know. I didn't want to talk about how Daddy wasn't really who I thought he was. I could tell she didn't either.

For a week straight, I did nothing except go to school and come home from school.

I ate cold cereal out of a box for breakfast. No warm banana waffles with maple syrup for me. I was not in the mood to cook.

I packed tuna-salad sandwiches with celery for lunch. Normally I hated celery because of its crunchy texture and stringy parts. But it felt okay now because I could bite down hard.

I didn't do my normal good job on homework assignments.

I didn't erase mistakes when I made them on math papers in class. Instead I just crossed them out, making my paper look messy.

Miss Johnson said, "Groovy, your work has become careless lately. This isn't like you."

I said, "Would you mind calling me Eleanor

from now on, please?"

She raised her left eyebrow like she'd suddenly discovered a new germ. Then she wrote something on a yellow sticky note. But I didn't care what it was.

I went around not bothering to talk to people. During lunch recess I sat by myself in Miss Johnson's class pretending to read a book I couldn't put down for one single minute.

"You cannot avoid the world forever," she told me as she left for the teacher's lounge.

At home I didn't read or watch TV. Not even the cooking shows.

I didn't cut roses out of Mama's garden to put on the table and fill the house with good smells.

I didn't even make chocolate-covered strawberries.

Luis called. "Can you bring another batch?" he asked on the answering machine.

"No, I cannot," I told the telephone. I didn't call back.

Marisol called. "I can't find you at school

lately. Are you home sick? Felix wants to know what you found at the bank," she told the answering machine.

"Nothing," I told the telephone. I didn't call her back either.

I just sat around. I told myself, *You probably wouldn't have been able to sell enough strawberries to even buy a professional apron or white chef's hat.*

By the weekend, Mama took notice.

"You need something to motivate you," she told me.

"Like what?" I asked, even though I didn't feel like being motivated.

"You need to start making lists. It's the only way to get through a day." Mama walked to the kitchen and found a pencil and pad of paper. She handed them to me and stood next to the couch. She was dressed for work, ready to make her clients beautiful.

I sat up slightly.

She sighed her sigh that means she is trying to

be patient but is about to lose her patience.

So I sat up just a little more.

"First, and most important, consult the newspaper to see what the planets have in store for you. Then make your list." She opened the paper that was lying on the coffee table to the section with the horoscopes and folded it back, smoothing the creases perfectly. "This is so you have time to get everything done. Be sure to put a check mark next to each thing as you finish it. That way, you can see your progress. Feel your accomplishments."

I looked up at her.

"Think about what you want to do today, baby. Think about how you can make your dream come true. Write everything down. You'll feel better." Mama stood over me for a minute with a supercheery smile, like a cheerleader ready to do a C jump. Then she kissed the top of my head and walked to the front door. "I'll be back for lunch early today. I'm not that busy for a Saturday. Why don't you make us some of those sloppy joes you like? The ones with the sweet onions."

"Maybe."

She waved over her head, sparkles and glitter shining from every finger. "Good then. Love you!"

As soon as she closed the door, the doorbell rang. I looked around to see if she'd forgotten her black bag of supplies, but it was nowhere.

When I opened the door, Frankie stood there holding the empty trays I'd used to carry my chocolate-covered strawberries to the Swallow.

"Hey, Groovy," he said. "Luis asked me to give these to you. He thought you might need them to bring over a new batch."

I took the trays from him. Then I said, "I'm going by *Eleanor* now."

He looked at me real serious for a minute, and then said, "Okay."

"Thanks for the trays," I told him. "I gotta go. I'll see ya."

"Okay," he said again.

I closed the door and set the trays in the kitchen.

Then I sat down on the couch and looked at the pad of paper Mama had given me to make my list.

I counted the lines on it. Twenty-four.

I folded the top sheet into a paper airplane and flew it into the kitchen. I didn't pick it up.

After a real long time I made my list:

   1. *Eat breakfast.*
   2. *Get dressed.*

There was nothing else I needed to do.

And I absolutely was *not* going to cook sloppy joes for lunch. Not today or ever again.

HOW TO MAKE A LIST

Mama started asking to see my lists.

"I want to discuss your progress," she told me, like she was running a parent-teacher conference at school.

So sometimes I had to cheat. I'd write down the day as it happened, things like *brush teeth* and *clip fingernails. Go to school, come home from school.* I'd place a check mark next to them like I'd really thought about my day and planned them all along.

But Mama said she wanted me to write down more *important* things than routine tasks. Things like learning how to paint desert landscapes with barrel cacti and purple-orange sunsets by number. Or something really valuable like memorizing the constellations. Not to mention filling the order from Luis because, yes, he was still asking for another tray of strawberries, in case you hadn't heard his messages.

We sat at the kitchen table for breakfast before school one day, going over my progress and the lists I'd written. Mama had made burned toast and juice, but neither of us was eating.

"How about having a dinner party this week?" she said. "Your list could be something like, 'Plan menu, shop, cook.' You could invite Frankie and Luis."

"I'm not in the mood," I said.

"Hmmm," said Mama. She took little sips of juice. Finally she stood up. "Well, at least listen to your messages from yesterday. I don't know why you can't answer the phone anymore."

"Maybe I wasn't here when the phone rang," I said.

Mama frowned. Then she pressed the *play messages* button on the machine.

The sound of Luis's voice filled the room: "Hi, Eleanor. It's Luis again. We've run out of your strawberries. Frankie said he brought back your trays. Why don't you bring us some more? People are asking for them."

I glanced at Mama, feeling startled to hear someone actually call me Eleanor. I figured Frankie must have told him.

Then the next message: "Hey," Frankie's voice started. "It's Frankie. Call me back."

Marisol's message was after that: "Hello? This is Marisol." A long pause, then, "I was just wondering if you could come over to the restaurant. Well, okay. See ya."

I sighed and pulled myself out of the chair to stand up, trying my best to convince Mama I'd be acting like my normal self any second now. But the truth was, I still didn't care about talking to anyone or making chocolate-covered strawberries.

The phone rang. Mama picked it up with a look on her face that said, *See? I'm sure this is someone for you now.*

I heard her say hello, but then she walked quickly into the laundry room.

For a long time, she didn't speak. Then she said, "Yes."

Then, "Okay."

Then, "I understand."

Then, "Okay," again.

When she hung up, she stayed in the laundry room.

I yelled to her, "Who was that?"

Mama walked slowly into the kitchen. "You know, with all this hot weather, I believe I need a deep-conditioning treatment for my hair. It feels so *dry* suddenly." She walked past me. "Bye," she said.

And she left for work without kissing me on the head good-bye or telling me to have a good day like she usually does.

That's how I knew that whoever had called

had probably given her some kind of news about Daddy.

I thought about writing him a letter after she left for work. So I could ask him why he did it.

I made a list. It read:

1. *Write Daddy.*

But I didn't.

CINNAMON CHURRO
BUT NO ROOT BEER

Spring break started off hotter than ever. It was as if March had gotten confused with August.

"You need to have some *fun*, baby," Mama finally told me. "It's Swallows Week, after all. Everyone's getting ready for the swallows to return. There's even a band playing today. Why don't you go see Frankie at the shop?"

"Maybe," I answered. I was feeling tired from all my list making and sitting around.

"I was afraid of this." She looked me over, her

hands firm on her hips. "I think it's time for some-thing big. How about a color change? Maybe a nice red. Not a bright red, just a soft one, to bring out your eyes more." She ran her fingers through my hair, pulling at the tangles.

"No, Mama. I don't want red hair."

"Don't say no right away. Think about it. I'll bring home some color samples." She packed her bag with brushes and shampoos. "Might be just what you need, baby."

"I'm *not* changing my hair," I told her.

"We'll talk about it some more later," she called to me as she walked out the door. "I'll be home for lunch."

You could not stop my mother from doing a makeover on someone if you tried. What was she thinking, though? I barely felt like myself now. How would dyeing my hair help?

After a while, I decided that walking to the Swallow for a cinnamon churro would be okay because I wouldn't get anything extra. Not a root beer, or an Icee. Nothing that would remind me of anything nice.

I got some money and walked along the docks to the shop. The high tide lapped at the pylons, covering all but a few sharp mussels. They twinkled brightly from the sunlight catching their wet black shells. The smell of fish and sand and sunscreen had settled permanently into the wood I walked on.

When I got to the shop, three new sketches of swallows lined the sidewalk: a bird getting ready to take off, a bird lifting into the air, a bird in full flight. I wondered what was the limit of Marisol's drawing talent. I knew, looking at the sketches, that she'd be famous someday. I'd say, "Oh, yes, Marisol Cruz, I knew her when she first started out."

In the distance, I could see Frankie standing at the end of the dock. So I headed down to meet him.

"How did you know I was coming?" I asked as I walked up.

"I didn't," he answered. "I was watching that boat." He pointed to a big green and white sailboat named *Sea Fever*. The crew was getting ready to throw off their lines and head out to sea.

"You never told me what you found at the bank," he said.

I sighed. "Nothing."

"The safe-deposit box was empty?"

"I mean my daddy wrote in the bank book that he'd taken all the money, so yes, there was nothing worth finding inside."

Frankie nodded like he sort of thought that's what would've been in there. "Hmmm," he said. Then he turned back to the *Sea Fever*. I could tell by the way he stuffed his hands into his pockets that he wouldn't ask me any more questions, and I felt relieved.

We watched the boat's sails luff in the wind. Four seagulls circled the top of the mast so closely I wondered if it had been smeared with peanut butter.

That's when I saw him standing on the bow, looking out toward the sun: Mr. Tom in his yellow jacket.

"So long, Skip!" yelled the man standing on the dock next to the sailboat. He saluted his right hand in the direction of Mr. Tom.

"His name is Skip?" Frankie asked the man, as we hurried to where he was.

"Well, no," he replied. "That's just his nickname. His real name is Tom Harris. Best sailor in the Pacific. I served with him for ten years when we were in the navy."

I realized then I'd been wrong about thinking Mr. Tom had found the yellow coat the afternoon we saw him sitting on the jetty. *Skip* was a nickname I just didn't know about.

The man winked at us and smiled. "You here to say good-bye too?"

"Where's he going?" Frankie asked.

"To the channel island of Santa Catalina. Thirty-three degrees longitude and one hundred eighteen degrees latitude," the man told us. "Great place to fish. Great place to retire. He's going across with a friend of mine." He nodded slowly. "Yep, Skip came into a trailer over there. Just worked out for him finally," he told us, like he was trying to believe Mr. Tom's good fortune himself.

"Well"—he smiled—"everyone deserves a little good luck at least once in their lives—right, mates?"

Mr. Tom came around from the bow of the sailboat, his yellow jacket flapping in the wind around his legs. He looked a lot different from before, like he'd gotten a bath, and he wore white tennis shoes instead of his blue flip-flops. I wondered if he remembered who we were.

"What do you two want?" he asked, looking right at me.

"I don't want anything," I heard myself say. Because it was true. I didn't even want a churro anymore.

I glanced around then to see if anyone else was there, someone who might know Mama and tell her that I was talking to Mr. Tom.

"I guess we should say good-bye," Frankie said to him. And I thought he sounded a little sad to see him go.

Mr. Tom waved to the captain and put his first finger up, like he was asking for just one more minute before they left. Then he stepped closer to the edge of the boat, holding tight to the halyard. He didn't say good-bye back to Frankie. He didn't even look at Frankie.

Instead, it was like he didn't hear him at all because he kept his eyes right on me. Like we were the only two people in the whole world.

Mr. Tom shook his head. "You don't want what Frankie has. All that anger will turn you to stone."

I stepped back. Frankie raised his eyebrows at me, like he was wondering what was going on.

"I tried to tell you that before," Mr. Tom said, looking at me long and hard. "I tried to tell you both." He pushed his lips tight, seeing into my eyes like he knew me better than even my mama.

Now it is a funny thing about people who can see deep into you. Past your clothes and your face. Past what you say.

They know things about you that you haven't told them in words. Mama says it's because they listen better than everyone else.

I never knew what she was talking about until that very minute. Because suddenly I was sure Mr. Tom could see the feelings in me, the same way he had seen them in Frankie that afternoon on the jetty after he'd gotten the letter from his mama.

And then, just as I thought he was about to walk away from us and into his new life on the island, he jumped down off the boat onto the dock.

He walked over to me until there was practically no space between us. The smell of Ivory soap drifted from him. I noticed his fingernails had been trimmed and cleaned. Even so, an uneasy feeling settled into my stomach.

But then, the more I looked at him, with his nickname there on his coat and his smooth shark's-tooth necklace around his neck, the more I just knew there was nothing to be afraid of.

He reached to touch my shoulder and stared into my eyes, then squinted. Not from the sun, which was shining hard off the ocean just then. But from the story he must have seen, and the girl

I knew I would become if I chose not to forgive. Because I could see that he knew all about people not showing forgiveness from his wrinkled-sheet face, the way his eyebrows slanted down on the edges, the sadness they whispered.

And without telling me any of this out loud, my heart knew what he was saying by the way he took his time, as if he was sending me a silent message saying, *No more.*

I knew it just as sure as those humpback whales know the way to Mexico when they swim there each winter to find a family.

But even though I felt his message, I saw myself turn away while the rest of those whales kept straight on the path.

I stepped back. Away from Mr. Tom. Far enough so he wouldn't see that I didn't want to forgive my daddy. Even if it did bring me personal suffering like he said it would.

VACATION MEMORY

Frankie and I silently watched the *Sea Fever* sail out of the harbor that day.

I could tell he was thinking about what Mr. Tom had said to me by the look on his face because he seemed real serious. It was the same look he had when his mama came back to the Swallow looking for him.

As for me, I kept thinking about the summer I'd turned nine. I remembered when Mama and Daddy and I took a week off to drive to the Grand Canyon so I could see more of the world, and they could get away from it all.

Before we left, we'd gone to the library to get maps and booklets about the sites, and the phone numbers of the different motels where we'd stay. Mama made sure they all had a pool, too, so I could practice holding my breath underwater, and she and Daddy could relax alongside it. She said that that was the number-one question to motel owners: "Do you have a nice pool?" Because people want to find out about the place before they get there.

By the fifth day, though, after seeing Mother Nature's Grand Canyon from the back of a mule while riding down a steep path, Mama told Daddy she'd seen all the rocks and ravines she could take for one vacation. So the two of us went shopping. We made our way toward a little town that sold handmade Indian blankets and God's eyes, which were pieces of yarn wrapped in a diamond shape around two sticks. Mama said the God's eyes brought good luck.

I remember we got lost after she took a right turn down a dirt road that had potholes and rocks the size of basketballs lying along the sides, instead of taking a left turn at the Gravel Stop store and gas station, like I told her to.

I watched dirt clouds rise and circle up in the sky then settle back to the ground as our car made its way, and Mama started to get real mad.

"We're out in the middle of nowhere!" she yelled to me, wiping bits of dust from her lips and teeth.

"We have to be *somewhere*," I told her.

"This isn't even on the map." She pushed the gas pedal harder.

I remember how hot it was and how it seemed that nothing could survive with the rocks and dust and sun but lizards and weeds. I wondered how anyone could've made the road we were on in the first place.

"Slow down, Mama!" I told her.

"For what, baby? There's nothing out here but nothing."

Then I saw a small sign. There were red painted letters on cracked splintery wood that read, NEXT

TOWN—27 MILES, with an arrow pointing in the opposite direction.

I yelled at her to stop.

She put on the brakes hard, and our car slid sideways.

We stopped next to a clump of thorny ocotillo cactus and pieces of green broken glass left from an empty soda bottle.

The dust pushed around us, under us, above us, and rose up in front of our car in the shape of a mushroom. Black crows yelled above in the sky, circling, waiting to see if we'd be their next meal.

"What in the *world*?" Mama gasped, bending her neck to see out the window.

"You almost hit it, Mama. I told you to slow down."

She got out of our car, leaving her door open and the engine running, and walked up to that sign, good and close, to double-check that we were reading it right.

I leaned my head out my window to watch her. Tiny grains of soft red-brown dust landed on my eyelashes and cheeks.

"See!" she yelled, with her hands in the air. Her pink bandanna, tied around her hair to keep the desert air from drying it out, waved in the breeze. "The sign is telling us to go back in the other direction, baby! It's a good thing we saw this. Otherwise we'd be long lost in another hour or so!"

Well, that's exactly what Mr. Tom was. A sign to point me in the right direction. To tell me to have mercy toward Daddy.

And for a half second I thought, *I should do what that sign says. I should forgive Daddy.* I felt it deep inside, like it'd been put there when I wasn't watching in a message Pastor Ken had given us one Sunday. Or maybe it'd been there all along, like something I was born with. Like something that comes up when you need it to tell you, *In case you don't know, this is the right thing to do. No matter how mad you feel.*

But instead I ignored it. I didn't pay any attention to that sign.

STRAWBERRIES GONE BAD

"All this hot weather isn't helping your strawberries stay fresh," Mama said to me the next day at breakfast. "I hate to see what our summer will be like if this is only spring. Do you wanna do something with these? Soon they'll be rotted."

I shrugged. "I don't know." I did and I didn't.

Mama looked me over. "Well, I won't order any more from the fruit market until you're . . . ready."

She wiped up the kitchen counter with a pink sponge. I could tell she was waiting for me to explain why five dozen strawberries weren't dipped in chocolate yet. Why my Fortune 500 company wasn't making a profit at the moment.

"I guess I'll have to think up another way to use them, then," Mama finally said.

Which was fine with me.

THE SCOUT

I walked down to the Swallow the next day. I didn't bother making a list that morning, and Mama seemed not to notice I was directionless for once. I steered clear from the jetty rocks where Daddy and I used to sit while having our usual morning hot-chocolate talks.

Frankie, Marisol, and Felix were sitting on the yellow bench outside the shop when I got there, drinking Oranginas and sorting fishing hooks into boxes. A small parade of young children on tricycles alongside their mothers inched slowly in a zigzag line past the front of the Swallow. They

waved triangle-shaped red flags that read, WEL-
COME SWALLOWS.

"Hey," I said as I walked up.

"Hey," Frankie told me.

"Hey," said Marisol.

"Frankie said you don't wanna talk about
not finding any treasure at the bank," said Felix.
"Sorry, though."

"It's okay," I told him. I looked at Frankie,
and he shrugged as if to say, *I told him not to
bring it up.*

"The scout is here. The first swallow. She flew
in early this morning to look things over and find
the usual spots where the rest of the flock will
come to," Frankie told me.

"Really?" I asked.

"Wanna see her?" Felix stood up.

"Yeah," I answered, and we all followed
Frankie behind the shop to where a few olive
trees stood. They were at least a hundred years
old, but still gave a harvest of medium-size dark-
gray olives each year. Nobody ever picked them

up, though, leaving them as a free-for-all for birds and mice. Mist gathered on the ground, covering dead leaves and shriveling olives and dirt.

"Right there. In the middle of that tree. See her?" Frankie pointed to the highest branch. Sunlight reached through the trees, crowning her in a goldish yellow morning light.

Sure enough, she had come. Her dark-brown feathers pressed against her body at the sound of our voices.

"She's beautiful," Marisol said.

"She's early," I added.

"About a week, actually," Frankie said. "She'll fly back in a day or two and then guide the rest of the flock here. Probably by the end of the week."

"That soon?" Marisol asked. She looked sad, like maybe the scout would leave before she'd had the chance to sketch her.

"Yeah." Frankie shaded his eyes from the sun to get a better look at her.

"She came alone?" I asked, knowing that usually the swallow scouts flew in pairs.

"Yeah. Luis says it's not uncommon. He's seen it before," Frankie told us.

"I'm gonna go get my sketchbook. I'll see you guys later," Marisol said. "Come on, Felix."

"I know where it is," said Felix. "I seen it in your room on top of your dresser next to the lamp. Can I carry it?"

We watched them walk toward their house while Marisol explained the differences between chalk and charcoal, and which paper was best for each.

"There's something else, too," Frankie said to me as they finally turned the corner.

I looked at Frankie. "What?"

"The Fish and Game Commission halted all big fishing for the next two years. They said there's been too much harvesting and the oceans need time to replenish themselves. It's been in all the papers."

"Oh," I said, not sure what this had to do with the scout.

Frankie nodded and looked at the ground awhile.

"So?" I asked him.

"So Luis got a letter from my mom. And she sent him this white envelope." He bent over as if he was having a stomach cramp. Then he looked up at the scout.

I watched him study her like maybe she knew something he wanted to understand, and I remembered the white envelope his mama had tried to give him the day she came, how he'd refused to take it then and how I'd imagined it had been full of photos.

"I guess they're coming back this summer to live here. Until the restrictions are lifted at least," Frankie told the scout. He looked at me then, and I saw something quiet and calm in his eyes. Something happyish, but scared at the same time.

"There was a copy of her green card in that white envelope. She wanted me to have it when she came, but I wouldn't take it." He gripped a roll of Tums tight in his left hand. "Luis said she wanted me to hold it for her," he said. "That all this time, she'd been here in the U.S. on only a work visa, and the government wouldn't renew it anymore."

"What's a green card?"

"It lets her live here forever, even though she was born in Mexico. I guess they've been fishing there until the paperwork came through. Her letter said she wanted me to stay here to go to school. That because I was born here, I was already a citizen and it would be better for me." His eyes found the swallow again and he watched her for a long time. Then he turned back to me and nodded as if to say, *Well, things are changing around here, and I'm not sure I want them to.*

"Did you know about this?" I asked him.

"No." Frankie shook his head. "I don't feel very well."

I didn't say anything then. I wanted to tell him that her getting a green card was good news. That her waiting all this time for the paperwork to come through explained the mystery of why she left with only a carry-on. But I couldn't. I didn't want to risk making him unwrap another roll of Tums.

WHITE CHOCOLATE

By the end of the week, I'd memorized most of the main constellations in the night sky and checked that off my list. Cassiopeia, Hercules, Ursa Major and Minor.

Mama gave me one of her smiles. The one that said, *I knew you could do it if you tried*.

It was easy to find time to memorize things, seeing as how I hadn't left the house since hearing the news of Frankie's mama coming back. Not to mention my days were no longer taken up by cooking of any kind whatsoever.

I'd say to Mama, "Maybe tomorrow," meaning, maybe tomorrow I'd be back to normal and we'd have something we could actually *eat* for dinner instead of one of her mystery casseroles she'd taken to making. I didn't bother telling her that you can't mix hamburger meat with leftover chicken in the same recipe. Or that cheese and crackers do not actually count as a meal, even if served with milk.

Then, after a completely boring lunch of two microwaved slices of cheese pizza, which take no cooking skills to make, just as I was about to settle onto the couch for another day of nothing mixed with sulking, the doorbell rang.

"Marisol's bossy," Felix said to me when I opened the door. He was wearing one of those T-shirts where you copy a photograph onto the fabric. It was a picture of his sister's art. I could tell because her initials were written in black letters in the bottom right corner.

"Yeah," he said. "I don't know if I want to be her assistant anymore."

I looked at him. I knew how he felt, not wanting

to do much of anything myself lately.

"She told me to come get you," Felix said. "She left you a message about it on the phone. You're supposed to come with me. I'm not supposed to tell you what it's about."

"Tell your sister I'll see her some other time. I'm kind of tired."

"If you don't come, she'll get mad at me." Felix's jaw tightened, and for a minute I thought he might start crying.

I didn't want to go with Felix, but with tears building up in his eyes by the second, I thought I'd better save him from Marisol getting mad— which I could imagine happening, she being the sort of girl she was.

Felix held out his hand. "Come see," he said.

I took his hand and we walked together toward his father's restaurant. You would think that the sunniness outside would've helped to brighten my mood, but no. It only made it worse. I thought, *Okay, I'm coming. But this better be good. It better be super-extremely seriously good.*

When we got to the restaurant, Felix led me to where Marisol sat at a small table covered by a red cloth. The dining part of the restaurant was empty except for the three of us. I could hear someone washing dishes in the kitchen, pots banging, water turning on and off.

"Hey," Marisol said.

"Hi," I told her.

"How's it going?" she asked.

I shrugged. "Fine."

She said, "So Frankie said you changed your name."

"Well, technically it's my real name."

"Yeah? I was thinking that since I'm an up-and-coming artist and all, I might do that too. Like the movie stars do. I've got a list going of possibilities. I'm still in the brainstorming stage."

"Good," I said.

She nodded, agreeing. Then she suddenly stared at the table next to us. "That's weird," she said in a quiet voice.

Felix and I looked at the table. Her sketchbook

lay on top with two charcoal pencils alongside it. I could see where a third pencil lay on the floor nearby.

"One of my pencils just rolled off that table. They were in a pile together, and now one of them is on the floor." Marisol took a step toward the table, and then a step back, like she decided she wouldn't go over there after all. "Weird," she said again.

"You want me to pick it up?" Felix asked, like he would be doing something very important that took a lot of skill.

Marisol thought for a second. "I guess so, yeah." Her forehead scrunched up as she bent down to look under the table and search the floor.

Felix picked up the charcoal pencil and placed it alongside the other two. "Marisol doesn't like her stuff messed up," he told me. "I know how she likes it." He grinned at his sister.

"Maybe a breeze made it roll off," I told Marisol.

She bit her lip. "Maybe."

"Maybe it was always *on* the floor," Felix said.

Marisol rolled her eyes. "I *know* where I put my pencils," she said. Then she shrugged and carefully lifted a white napkin covering a plate that was sitting on the table.

On the plate were three strawberries covered in chocolate. They weren't as big as the ones I used but, other than that, they looked like I'd made them.

Felix leaned in close to get a good look. And at first I didn't see what he was looking at, the small figures, not more than an inch long: two tri angles carefully drawn in white chocolate, and in the middle, a shape like a teardrop. It was a body and two wings. Marisol had drawn a tiny bird on each of the strawberries using white chocolate.

"I did it with a toothpick," she said. "It wasn't hard."

I looked up at her. I was about to tell her how much better the strawberries were with the drawings on them. How it made them seem even more special. How using white chocolate to draw over the dark chocolate looked . . . beautiful.

Then she said, "I thought you might like them. I thought, after seeing them, you might want to start up again. I saw there weren't any this week or last week. Luis said you stopped bringing them in. You can use my design if you want."

I'm here to tell you there was nothing more I wanted just then. Seeing Marisol's birds on the strawberries gave me a hopeful feeling I hadn't had for a long time.

So I nodded to her that I would be using her design.

And I smiled like someone who couldn't wait to get started.

PETROCHELIDON PYRRHONOTA

～

I marched straight to the Swallow after that. If you could've seen me walking, you would've known by the way I swung my arms and smiled that I was feeling just about back to normal. I made my list of supplies in my head as I walked: *three* kinds of chocolate, toothpicks, strawberries; I needed it all.

"Where have you been?" Frankie asked when he saw me. "A few of the swallows have arrived. We've seen them flying overhead."

"Already?" I asked. Then I noticed a small crowd of people standing on the sidewalk, armed with cameras and binoculars.

"We think the rest will come today. They should be here anytime now." His eyes were shining. "Want some binoculars?"

I nodded. "Thanks. How do you know they'll be here today?" I asked as we joined the crowd.

A tall kid with blondish hair wearing an official-looking vest stepped close to us. "I'm a bird tracker," he told us, grinning. "My sources identified the swallows leaving Goya, Argentina, in mid-February—about a month ago. By the time they get here, they'll have flown seventy-five hundred miles." He checked his watch. "I expect they'll be here anytime."

Frankie beamed. "A bird tracker? You wouldn't happen to know their official species name, would you?"

"*Petrochelidon pyrrhonota,*" he said slowly. "But we call them cliff swallows. It's a lot easier. Wanna see their picture?" He whisked a small booklet from one of his vest pockets and opened to a drawing of a swallow.

Our heads bent over the page. "That's them," Frankie said.

Luis found us after that.

"Hello, Hugh," he said to the bird tracker. "I was wondering if you'd make it again this year. How's your bird book coming?"

Hugh smiled proudly. "I was just showing it off."

"How long have you been studying birds?" Frankie asked him.

"Since I was ten," Hugh told us. "I'm twelve now. I went to a bird-sanctuary camp that summer. Did you know birds have special air sacs that make up twenty percent of their body?"

"Yeah?" said Frankie.

Hugh nodded. "That's what keeps their lungs inflated so they fly easy. I got lots more stuff about them in here." He held up his booklet. "You guys want one?"

I looked at Frankie. I knew he did.

"Thanks," Frankie told him.

The four of us stood together, waiting, watching every corner of the sky while Hugh recited more facts. Bird heartbeat rates. Hollow-bone skeletal structures. Airfoil wings.

Of course, Frankie saw the swallows first. "There they are!" he shouted, pointing southeast past the hills.

In the distance, a small dark blur of birds moved toward us, then shifted, a slight turn to the right, like a late-afternoon cloud forming and changing into shapes. They flew over houses, trees, hills, everything; knowing their way home.

The swallows had made the incredible journey north, thousands of miles from south of the equator itself, over the Gulf of Mexico, to the San Juan Capistrano Mission and the area around it. The sound of their chirping fell across us as some of them slowed to perch on the sign above, settling in next to one another like they had preassigned seats in a math class.

And I decided it was the best thing I'd seen in

a long time, with all those birds getting along so well.

"They know where to come, even after being gone so long," Frankie told me proudly.

"It's in their blood," Luis added. He was taking pictures right and left.

I crowded closer to let in more people who'd just arrived. They waved flags and pointed upward. A dad next to me lifted his little boy onto his shoulders so he could get a better look, while Hugh whispered words into a small tape recorder. I could see Marisol and Felix across the street, a sketchbook glued to Marisol's right hand, a piece of charcoal in her left. She was flipping back and forth between pages, drawing the whole thing while Felix waved to us.

We tried to be quiet and not disturb the birds, but the excitement was hard to keep hushed. I could even feel my own cheerfulness moving around inside just a little. Like it had been asleep for a while but was now waking.

"Help me pass out these pamphlets," Luis said

to me, and handed over a small stack of papers. "They tell the story of the swallows, how long they've been coming, where they start off, things like that." He smiled. "I put some of my best photos in there from last year."

"See what I mean?" Frankie turned to me, his face looking like he, more than anyone in the world, knew about those birds. "They always come back. Without you having to ask them."

A PILLOWCASE FULL
OF HALLOWEEN CANDY

Luis had a record sales day.

By the end of the afternoon, he didn't even have any tacos left to sell. He said it was like that every year the day the swallows returned.

I stayed around later than usual to help him and Frankie with the rush. I swept and bagged stuff for customers after Luis rang them up. Frankie worked in the back freezer section, organizing ice and cold drinks for people.

As I was shaking out a white plastic bag from its flatness and stuck-togetherness, I noticed Mr.

Tom waiting in line with a basket full of supplies. I looked away from him quickly. My face grew hot remembering the day he'd jumped off the *Sea Fever* to talk to me on the docks, how it had felt like he'd been able to see right into me. *Please don't talk to me again. Not in front of Luis.*

His tanned, wrinkled hands slid the basket slowly onto the counter as he made his way to the checkout. I tried to pay close attention to the stuff inside, like those things were the most important things someone could buy in the whole world.

What was in the basket: a box of worms that were still alive; a can of cream soda; two ham sandwiches without cheese; clear fishing line; AAA batteries; wire cutters; Chap Stick; duct tape; fishhooks in different sizes; a pair of pliers.

"Going back to the island tomorrow, Tom?" Luis asked him.

My eyes quickly darted toward Mr. Tom, as if they had a mind of their own. Like they couldn't help it and he was a magnet and they were iron.

Mr. Tom nodded at the ground.

"I heard you were back for the day. Came to get some supplies?" Luis talked soft and low. He took the bag from me, putting the things inside without holding them over the checkout scanner.

I looked up to Luis to tell him he must've forgotten, but he shook his head just a little, before I could say anything, so no one else would see but me. And I realized he was not going to make Mr. Tom pay.

Mr. Tom walked to the end of the counter. Luis handed him his bag, and Mr. Tom nodded again like he was saying thank you.

He walked to the front door and stopped. His white grocery bag hung from his hand like a pillowcase full of Halloween candy. "Hey," he said, turning back. "You tell your dad thank you. Tell him I'm all settled." He smiled the tiniest half smile then, which I'd never seen him do before. Like now he was someone who had things to smile about.

I looked at Luis, confused. *Was he talking to me?*

Luis's eyebrows scrunched up. I could tell he had no idea either.

We waited for him to say something else. Instead, he left, with the bells on the door ringing good-bye as it swung shut.

"He must not remember my daddy's . . . situation," I told Luis, not mentioning the word jail on purpose. I shrugged. Mama was right, Mr. Tom was crazy.

"No . . ." Luis's voice trailed off. He put his hand on his chin, thinking, remembering something. "I think he knows about your dad." He tapped his finger on his jaw, like he was trying to push out what he wanted from his memory. "Well, anyway," he said finally.

"You don't make him pay for supplies?" I asked Luis.

"He doesn't have any money."

"But he could get a job," I told him.

"Not Tom." He pressed the drawer of the cash register closed, like he did after each sale. Even though he had not technically made a sale.

"So you just give him stuff when he comes through? Whatever he wants?"

"I didn't need those things. Plus, it wasn't much." Luis reached to the next basket and started ringing up a customer who'd walked up. She was wearing a big straw hat and a T-shirt with a picture of a swallow on it.

"But he won't ever pay you back," I told Luis. I'd had experience about not getting paid back.

Luis leaned closer to me. Then, in a quiet voice so only I could hear, he said, "People are just who they are."

And then he smiled at the lady waiting in line and continued ringing her up.

I got another white bag ready. And I waited for him to hand me her things after he scanned them through the checkout.

CARD GAME

~~

It took me a while to get home that day. Everyone was celebrating, having picnics and gathering together. I saw my teacher sitting on the grass. "Hey, Miss Johnson!" I waved from the sidewalk.

"Hello, Eleanor!" she shouted back. "What a perfect day, don't you agree?"

"Yes, I do," I told her, because it almost was, between Marisol's surprise and the swallows coming back.

When I reached the roses lining our yard, I heard the phone ringing through the kitchen window, hurrying me inside.

I grabbed it on the sixth ring. "Hello, Mama," I said, knowing it would be her checking on me as usual. "I'm sorry I'm late getting home for dinner. I was helping out at the Swallow. Did you eat already?" I looked around the kitchen for one of Mama's dinners. Nothing was on the counter.

"Groovy, it's me." There was a pause, then, "It's your dad."

His voice sounded familiar to me, but different. Like something I knew, but didn't. A rush of thoughts came into my head at once. *Why did all of this have to happen? Why didn't you care about me?* But all I could say was, "Oh."

"I've been calling for hours," he told me. "I've been trying to reach you. Has your mother told you I've been trying to reach you?"

"They let you use the phone in jail?" I asked. *Didn't they have rules about that?*

"Officer Miguel thought that since today was normally visiting hours and all, that it would be okay to call since no one was visiting," he said, sounding sad.

"Oh."

"Groovy, knowing your mother, I'm sure she's explained everything to you by now."

"She did," I interrupted. I didn't want to hear it. I didn't want to listen to him admit the truth.

I waited. Silence. The phone felt hot on my ear. I wrapped the cord around my left fingers so tight, the ends turned bluish and numb.

"And also," I said, "please don't call me Groovy anymore. I'm going by *Eleanor* these days." I wanted him to know I didn't care about his nickname for me.

"I see," he answered, like he could tell I'd made up my mind and that I was real upset about the whole thing.

I waited again. I had nothing else to say. The kitchen faucet dripped loudly into an empty bottle of hair bleach lying in the sink.

"I'm sorry," he said after a while.

I wanted to tell him that that wasn't enough. That the whole point of the money was for me to decide how it was used. "I would've used that money to go to cooking school," I said, suddenly feeling full of energy.

He didn't answer. I could hear him breathing.

"Yeah," I said again. "That's what I would've done with it." A sadness rose up in me then that had nothing to do with missing cooking school and more to do with how apart I felt from him, how maybe it had always been that way.

"Well," I said, "I better go now."

"By the time you're ready to go to school, I'll have that money back in your account. I won't be in here forever. Haven't you read my letters?"

I remembered the mail Mama had stuffed into her pocket then, and realized it must have been for me. That he must've been trying to explain. It didn't matter, though. I already knew everything after going to the bank. I wrapped the phone cord around my other hand, wondering how long he would be there. Mr. Tom's words came back to me then. *You tell your dad thank you. Tell him I'm all settled.*

I heard myself say, "I saw Mr. Tom today, you know, that homeless man. He wanted me to tell you thank you. I guess he doesn't remember you're in jail," I explained, like obviously none of it made sense.

"Is that so?" His voice sounded calm.

"So you know what he's talking about?"

"It's nothing really. He won a bet, that's all."

"What kinda bet?"

"I had a client on the island a few months back, sold his mobile home for him. He paid me with a trailer. Said he couldn't afford the commission, that the trailer was worth the commission. But hell, what was I gonna do with a trailer? Tom won it from me in a card game. I guess I could've sold it, but he needed a place to live."

"*You* lost a card game?" I didn't believe it. He never even lost at go fish.

"Well, no. I actually let him win."

"Does Mama know about this?"

"Your mother?" he said. "No. Your mother doesn't know a thing. She would've had that place remodeled and sold in a week. Put that money in the bank." He sighed. "I probably should've told you both a lot of things. Done things differently. I know that now."

I could picture him then as he hung up the phone, nodding his head, how he'd bunch his lower lip up into the top one and nod. The same way he did whenever he made a big decision.

Like giving a trailer to Mr. Tom when he could've sold it for money.

A NICE TUNA FISH
CASSEROLE WITH PEAS

Mama came barreling loudly through the back door five minutes later, her black bag brimming with boxes of red hair dye. "Did you see the swallows?"

"You scared me, Mama!" I gasped, startled out of deep thought. I'd been thinking about everything Daddy had said, deciding whether or not to tell Mama about his call. How he seemed sad but peaceful, *different* today than I could ever remember. I could see how Mama would've been mad about him giving the trailer to Mr. Tom when he could've used that money, and why he didn't tell her about it. And even though selling the trailer would've been the smart thing to do, there was a part of me that felt glad he'd let Mr. Tom win it from him. There was something about Daddy giving away one of his last valuable possessions that made me feel he had goodness in him again.

"The paper said the swallows are ahead of schedule this year. They must know something we don't," Mama said.

"Maybe they got confused," I told her.

"Baby"—Mama put her hands on her hips—"Mother Nature does *not* get confused." She looked at me with her eyebrows scrunched up. Like maybe I'd come down with a fever that was sucking up all my common sense. I knew she was wondering how in the world a daughter of hers would not know this fact.

I shrugged. There was too much in my brain at once.

"Here they are," she said. "You can look through them and decide. I've been collecting different products." She picked up a box with a picture of a pretty girl on it who looked like a movie star. She had shiny red hair. "This one, in my *professional* opinion, would look best with your coloring."

"Mama, I told you before, I'm not changing my hair." I felt tired. Exhausted actually. I sat down at the table. My conversation with Daddy rang in my ears. I laid my head in the palms of my hands and closed my eyes. A picture of him nodding his head appeared. *I should've done things differently,* I heard him say.

"Maybe after dinner," she answered, smoothing my hair, her cool hands gentle and strong at the same time. "I thought *you* could make dinner tonight. Maybe a nice tuna fish casserole with peas."

She paused then with her hand on my head. Her body froze. "Did you feel that?" she said slowly.

"What?" I asked her.

"Don't move," she whispered. Her hand gripped my hair, pulling it a little.

"What?" I asked again.

"The light over the kitchen table just moved. Look."

I bent my head toward the light. "It's not moving," I said.

"It *was* moving," she answered. She let go of my hair and tiptoed around the table, inspecting the light carefully. Then she glanced around the rest of the kitchen. "It's all this hot weather," she told me as she quickly checked under the kitchen sink. I watched her go through the cardboard box of makeup samples and pink foam hair curlers she kept in the back for emergencies.

I rolled my eyes at her to let her know I thought she was crazy. "Mama, please. There's no such thing as hot weather causing earthquakes."

"Darn heat," she said.

I laid my head back on the kitchen table. Secrets were mounting up inside me: the day I went to the bank, talking to Daddy on the telephone, all these things Mama knew nothing about. I could feel them pushing, saying, *Tell her everything. Tell her about the trailer he gave away to Mr. Tom.*

A small throbbing started behind my eyes. "Mama, do you miss Daddy?"

She sighed. "Sometimes." She took a deep breath in, like she was getting ready to tell me something else.

I waited.

But nothing. Instead she walked through the open sliding glass door into the backyard, stepped over a lime lying on the grass beneath our lime tree, crossed to the edge of the small hill, and looked over the ocean in the distance. Her shoulders were stiff.

I got up from the table and followed, ready to tell her everything. Blades of damp grass stuck to the soles of my feet and in between my toes as I walked, my head pounding. A warm breeze caught my hair, sending it in all directions, reminding me of the inside of my brain, how everything felt strewn about since Daddy's call.

At the edge of the hill, the setting sun sparkled off the sea like rays of light filtering through a crystal doorknob onto Mama's face, making it glow in a soft way. She took my hand in hers and squeezed it three times. *I. Love. You.* Our code from when I was little. I smiled at the sea, at Mama's love coming through her hand into mine, at the breeze whizzing around the hills like a game of tag.

And that's when I saw it. A tiny, soft white wishing weed, from what used to be a dandelion, drifting through the sky toward the ocean, maybe twenty feet from us. It bounced on the air, light and cheery, like it had nothing better to do, and I wondered if Mama saw it too. It floated slowly in an *S* pattern for a l o n g time, like it was making sure I knew it was there. I remembered the day Daddy had been arrested. How he'd stepped on a dandelion in front of the police car, crushing it. And I thought, *This could be that same dandelion. Only it's not ruined after all. It's spreading its seeds so it can come back again. And this time it'll plant itself in a field, to be safe. This time it will do things differently.*

A miniature tear crept into the corner of my

eye then, thinking about Daddy, hoping he'd meant what he said. How it all seemed possible, that we could be a family again someday.

The wishing weed drifted in front of the sun for the slightest second, the orange and amber colors of the sky soaked through its transparent whiteness until it looked like it had been tie-dyed by the sun.

It reminded me of camping with Daddy last summer, just the two of us. How we'd woken up extra early and watched from our sleeping bags on the sand, looking at the sunrise shed pink and orange and yellow across our sky.

"Red sky at night, sailors' delight," Daddy had told me. "Red sky in morning, sailors take warning."

"What does it mean?" I'd asked.

"It means those fishermen out there should watch out for that storm coming in. But don't worry, you're safe here with me. Even so, we'd better heat up our breakfast before that rain comes. Beans again?" He'd smiled his beans-are-the-best-thing-in-the-world smile and lit a match under our campfire.

I'd dug my feet deep under the cool sand, knowing even before he'd said it that I was safe. That at that moment, beans would taste better than even chocolate cake. And that he loved me.

Later that week he'd surprised me and painted that same sunrise on my bedroom wall. You have never seen a prettier painting. In the bottom corner he wrote, *You are my sunshine.* Sometimes in the morning, when the light starts to come through my window, it looks like a real sunrise, promising good things.

And with all those thoughts of hopefulness mounting inside me, I decided to use the wishing weed.

I sent a wish for Frankie. For his mama to come back soon so he could be close to her again. Then I sent a wish for Mr. Tom to get back to his island with his supplies to *his* trailer.

By the way I stood there grinning, you would've thought I suddenly got the news I was on my way straight to cooking school, that the classes had been paid for somehow and I had my white apron and chef knives. My head still pounding, a lightness settled over me, emptying everything out but the warmth between Mama's and my hands, and the knowing about Daddy wanting to do things differently.

Because then I did it.

I sent a wish for me. About Daddy being able to sit with me on the jetty rocks again one day. And at first I was surprised about what I wished for after everything that had happened.

But it felt okay, and just a little bit free. Like I could finally rest.

The wishing weed hovered lightly as it came to the edge of the sea. Like it was waiting to see if I had anything else to send it.

But then it caught a fast breeze. And whirled upward in a half circle before it flew west.

And suddenly it was gone.

Because it needed to hurry up and deliver all my wishes.

FORKS + KNIVES = MONOPOLY DICE

Spring break ended and school started up again.

Miss Johnson assigned our class a five-hundred-word essay to be written about the swallows. "Nothing factual, though," she told us. "I want you to write from the heart. Tell me how the swallows make you feel. Maybe in a tall tale, or a personal narrative. Anything creative."

I could tell Frankie's essay would get an A by the way he already had his first paragraph finished before I'd even started.

Mama's horoscope predicted business as usual

for two days straight, while mine, she reported, was calling for change.

"It's referring to your hair," she insisted, to which I rolled my eyes. I didn't believe in astrology, but I knew encouragement when I heard it. It was time for me to come clean and tell her everything, even my wish for Daddy to come home.

And then, at 2:08 in the afternoon on Saturday, while Mama took a short break from the salon for lunch, and she and I were sharing a plate of bell-pepper-and-blue-corn nachos at José's Cantina, surrounded by Marisol's newest sketches hung on the walls, it happened.

"Mama," I said. "I have something to tell you."

She looked up at me, her eyes waiting. "Have you decided to start making your chocolate-covered strawberries again?" she asked.

"Yes, I have."

Mama smiled. "I was sure that a person with the name of Eleanor would figure a way to work things out." Her face turned soft, and it made me want to get up out of my chair and put my arms around her right there.

"Thanks, Mama, but that's not what I wanted to tell you. It's about Daddy." I went over my list in my head of where to start—the bank, the phone call, the trailer—when suddenly the forks and knives on our table started bouncing toward the edges, like a pair of dice does when they're thrown onto a Monopoly board.

The wooden chandelier swung above our heads.

Glasses on our table tipped over, spilling ice cubes and Coca-Cola into a brown bubbling puddle around our feet.

My heart skipped and then beat hard. Instantly my body filled with enough energy to jump a million feet high.

I heard the glass in the windows shaking, warning us to move away in case they shattered.

"Earthquake!" shouted Mama, her eyes as big as ever. And for a moment our bodies were stuck to our chairs, feeling what was happening.

"Quickly, baby," she told me, "try to get to the doorway. We'll be safe there!"

And she grabbed my arm like she had been waiting for this her whole life.

We ran to the door between the kitchen and the dining room, where strong wooden beams crossed into the stucco walls, and held on tight. A waitress coming from the kitchen dropped her tray, scattering corn chips on the floor.

Customers screamed.

Some tried to make their way outside, stumbling and tripping over nothing but air.

Marisol's sketches fell from the wall.

Dishes crashed to the floor.

"Everyone get away from the windows!" yelled Marisol's father. He ran quickly from person to person, helping them to safety. I watched as he helped a mother and her two little boys huddle under a nearby table.

"Hold on to me, baby!" Mama screamed.

"I am!" I yelled into the air. But she couldn't hear me.

Because without warning, a piece of white-washed stucco broke apart from the ceiling and fell, shattering loudly into tiny pieces of dust and sharp chalky edges around our feet.

Mama pulled me back tight. "Don't look," she told me. Which was like telling me not to breathe because who could close their eyes while dodging pieces of a falling ceiling?

She grabbed my shoulders and kissed me on the forehead beneath my bangs. And I knew she loved me more that second than any other by the way she kept her lips pressed firm to me for so long.

Then, just as suddenly as it had started, the earth stopped shaking, and the restaurant became quiet.

My heart beat so loudly, I was sure Mama could hear it too.

Our fingers gripped tight to the wooden beam, not ready to let go.

We kept waiting.

Watching.

Not daring to move yet.

Not trusting it was over.

Because who can trust a ground that shatters ceilings without warning?

Little by little, people walked back into the restaurant and came out from under tables. Some hugged each other. One lady cried.

"It's over. We're okay," said Marisol's father. He stood in the middle of the room looking relieved, his arms raised up and spread wide. "Thank you, Jesus," he told the ceiling.

I looked at Mama. Her eyes stared straight ahead like she was in shock. She had read all those books about being ready for an earthquake. But I could tell from looking at her that her reading hadn't prepared her for what she felt when it actually happened.

"Mama," I said, knowing that nothing seemed important anymore except the truth about me wanting Daddy home again. So I went straight to it.

"Last week in the backyard, I saw a wishing

weed." I spoke the words slow, to be sure she heard every one. "I wished for Daddy to come back. I miss him." I said it like a teacher does when she gives the homework assignment at the end of each day. Like it was just how things were.

She stood quiet. Pieces of her blond hair fell into her face, and splotches of red skin popped up on her neck like they do when she's nervous. And for a minute, I didn't know if she'd heard me.

"Mama?" I reached to touch her face.

She took my hand and held it to her cheek. Soft little tears came out of her eyes while she kissed my fingers. And I knew she'd understood everything by the way she waited, pulling me close to her and nodding, like she was going to say the exact same thing but I'd beaten her to it.

"I know, baby," she finally answered. And she kissed me so lightly on the face then, it felt as if sifted flour was dusting my skin.

SPAGHETTI OUT OF A JAR

Mama counted six aftershocks that evening when we got home, but I didn't feel any of them. With each one, she became more jittery.

"Did you feel that one, baby?" she asked me. "It was stronger than the last one."

"No, Mama," I told her. "It must be your imagination." I was busy opening all the kitchen cabinets, checking for glasses that might have fallen over, and worrying about how Daddy was after the earthquake. "Do you want me to make you some tea?" I asked her.

"Who can sit and drink tea at a time like this?"

she answered, and huffed out of the room.

A second later she yelled to me from the living room. "I knew I felt a tremor last week. Remember the kitchen light? You thought *that* was my imagination too."

I didn't answer her on purpose.

Frankie stopped in on us soon after. "Everything okay?" He peered through the front door. "I brought drinking water and the newspaper." He held them up. "Looks like you were lucky. No damage?"

"I'm still checking," said Mama, motioning him inside. "Will you help me move some of this furniture?" She showed him her emergency procedure checklist. "Number five says to move collectibles and special items away from windows."

"I doubt we'll have another one, but if it will make you feel more comfortable, then fine." Frankie stepped inside.

I rolled my eyes to say sorry, showing him I thought she was not her normal self right now.

For an hour he helped her move furniture

around our house like they were chess pieces. And Mama was in a championship tournament, carefully directing each piece to the best spot.

When she was finally satisfied, I poured us all a glass of water from the jug Frankie had brought.

"Did you count our water-bottle supply in the garage?" Mama asked me, holding the glass of water in her hand as if it were precious metal.

"We have twenty-nine jugs," I told her.

"Are they the large ones?" She waited.

"Yes, they're the large ones. The ones we got at the warehouse market." I wondered how she could have forgotten this, seeing as how she'd made the entire staff at the market help us out that day.

"Good," she answered.

"Says in the paper they're predicting another scorcher for tomorrow. I can't believe how hot it is." Frankie opened up to the weather section of the newspaper and handed it to Mama.

"Do *not* give me another prediction about

anything!" She held up her hand. "I don't wanna hear it."

And then she did something that made me stop and stare at her, like she had taken my real mama and she was an impostor. She stood up like what Frankie had said was the final straw and she'd made up her mind. Then she grabbed the newspaper out of his hand.

Marched into the kitchen.

And *threw it away.*

Frankie looked at me, his face wondering what was wrong.

I followed her to the kitchen. My body suddenly felt hot. "But how will you plan your days?" I asked her. "How will you know what to write on your lists without consulting your horoscope first?"

Mama gasped, like she couldn't believe I didn't already know her answer. Her neck was covered in new splotches. "These horoscopes aren't any good when they don't say anything about *unexpected events* or near misses with *death*!"

And her saying that, I knew she'd said everything.

That night for dinner, I made spaghetti out of the jar. But Mama wouldn't eat. Even after I heated it up for her twice. She said she had some thinking to do instead.

"I'm telling you, it's all this hot weather that brings on these quakes," she said. "I hope we get a cooling trend soon."

I explained to her again, like I always did, that there was no such thing as earthquake weather. That earthquakes just happened on their own.

And that this had been proven *scientifically*— by scientists.

But she pretended not to hear me.

SCRAMBLED EGGS

The fog rolled in after 9:00 that night, and with it came a calming that blanketed our backyard and house, telling us, *It's over now, close your eyes and rest. Things will be better tomorrow.*

We sat on lawn chairs while dampness collected around us. Next to me, Mama's hand tapped a slow rhythm of love onto mine. I told her everything I'd been holding back, and through the whole story, her face stayed soft. She listened calmly, every once in a while saying, "Oh, baby," or "What else."

After I'd confessed it all, she said, "Sometimes

things get sorted out in your head after a crisis."

I wasn't sure if her sorting out meant forgiving Daddy, or giving up astrology. I hoped it was both.

"Do you think Daddy's okay?" I said. "I mean, after the earthquake?" I watched her face carefully, hoping she wouldn't be mad I'd brought him up.

Her mouth became tight. She sat for a minute, like she was deciding something, and then she said, "Actually, I know he's okay. I called the police station when we got home from the restaurant. Officer Miguel said they had no damage. Except for a metal file cabinet falling over in the office, and a shattered window. They were lucky, too."

I looked at her in shock. "You *called*? Did you talk to Daddy?" It came as great news to me that Mama would think to check on Daddy. That it mattered to her if pieces of ceiling might have been crashing down around him, too.

Mama shook her head. "No, I didn't talk to him. But I asked Officer Miguel to tell him I called. And to let him know that you were all right."

I smiled at her.

"I didn't want him to worry about you." She sighed. Then she twisted her hands into a ball of knots so tight her knuckles looked as if they would come out of her skin. "Officer Miguel said the earthquake was a 4.8 on the Richter scale. Darn heat," she said.

"Is 4.8 high?"

"Well, it sure *felt* high!" She stood up, looking like she was going to start worrying about something again. "But he said there were no injuries reported. Just minor damage. And that because José's Cantina is so old, the stucco ceiling was bound to come loose sooner or later."

I shook my head, wondering just how old it was.

"He also told me your father's jail sentence is coming to an end. And in about a week he'll be out. Then he'll start serving his probation," Mama said.

"What will he have to do?" I asked.

"The judge will tell him. Probably some sort

of community service. *And*"—Mama turned toward me, planting her hands on her hips like she was about to give me some sort of order— "he'll have to pay you back that money." Her face was a mixture of anger and irritation. But there was also relief.

"It will be okay," I told her.

Mama looked over my head toward the sea and sighed.

When she patted my shoulder, I knew it was her way of agreeing with me, without saying it aloud. That her patting my shoulder was equal to, *It will be okay.*

Finally at 10:00, she suggested I make scrambled eggs and toast because they went with our mood, which, she said, was uncomplicated and simple. I felt things seemed uncomplicated too. So I used my two-eggs-plus-$\frac{1}{8}$-cup-of-milk recipe, and they came out just right.

As I lay in bed that night, I started a new page in my cooking notebook. I made a list of foods that reminded me of things. I decided that it was one thing to come up with perfect menus for situations, but also that certain foods could end up reminding people of things. Because from now on, scrambled eggs would always remind me of tonight, when Mama and I sat in lawn chairs in the fog, and I told her the whole story.

Like when people say, "Oh, this corn on the cob reminds me of the time we barbecued at Uncle Joe's last summer." That sort of thing. Or like that test doctors do where they say a word, and you're supposed to say the first thing that comes to mind. *Dog, cat. Night, day. Scrambled eggs, talking.*

My list:

> *scrambled eggs = talking to Mama in the fog*
> *chocolate-covered coconut candy = our house*
> *one of Luis's tacos = the swallows coming back*
> *white chocolate = Marisol*

Looking it over, I realized everyone's list would be different depending on their own memories.

I entitled it: *Foodology*.

Half the word coming from *food*, of course, and half coming from *astrology*. I decided that if you could look it up in the dictionary, it would say: *(noun) the study of food; the way certain foods remind people of things*.

I knew if there were such a word, I would be an expert in foodology.

CLEANUP ON AISLE TWO

I spent Sunday helping Luis and Frankie clean up the Swallow.

"We're lucky to have only sweeping and straightening to do," Luis told us as he bent down to sweep a pile of broken glass into a dustpan.

He didn't bother to count the new cracks in the tile floor, which ran from the front door to the back counter and curved around the freezer section where he kept the ice and sodas.

He said nobody noticed those anyway.

"And also," he said to me, "with everything that's happened, your supplies will be a day or two late getting here. But we should have them by the middle of the week." He smiled then like there was nothing else he'd rather say.

Frankie put me in charge of cleaning up aisle two, which was the cereal aisle, while he restacked cans of refried beans and soup, and organized boxes of rice.

I put the Corn Pops and the Frosted Flakes back into perfect rows on the shelf, thinking that the shop was a little like Mama's and my life. How sometimes it got messed up, and we had to straighten it out. But usually it turned out all right, even though we might have a crack in the floor. Or less money to remind us that it happened.

After everything was back in its place, Luis made us some of Aunt Regina's secret-recipe tacos and fresh lemonade, and told us to take a break. So Frankie and I sat on the yellow bench outside, eating our lunches and watching the morning fog lift off the harbor.

Gray-and-white seagulls hovered in the air by the jetty. In the distance a lone pelican flew over the sea, following a long line of white foam.

"Frankie," I said after a while, "I want to tell you something. I've decided it would be okay with me if my daddy came back after he gets out of jail. I miss him."

Frankie set his lunch on the bench and looked at me, his eyes wide. "How can you forgive him so easily? He took that money from you and lied."

"I know."

"He *lied* to you," he said again, like maybe I'd forgotten. "About taking that money."

"You're right. But I talked to him on the phone. I can tell he's really sorry."

"You *talked* to him? After everything he did?" Frankie looked away, like I'd slapped him on the face. And I could feel a funny stiffness between us that made him seem like he was all the way across that sea.

For a long time, neither of us said a word.

Finally I told him, "I know what he did was wrong. And I don't expect you to be nice to him or anything. But I hope you'll be respecting my feelings." I waited for Frankie to say something.

"It's really not that," he answered.

"What then?"

He sat looking at the ground for a long time. Sidewalk ants hurried beneath us in a crooked line, marching over one of Marisol's sketches to gather on a sticky area.

Finally he said, "You got the biggest heart I know. After everything that happened, it seems like you should be mad, but . . ." He stopped and quickly wiped away wetness from his eyes with the back of his hand. I could tell he didn't want me to notice. Then he said, "Sometimes I wish I was like that."

I knew he was talking about how he wanted to talk to his mama again, really talk to her. How it was like he was standing on a busy street and could see her on the other side. And all he had to do was figure out a way to dodge those speeding cars between them without getting hurt.

I moved closer to him and put my arm around his shoulders. I waited for a while. Then I breathed in deep. The way Mama does so that everybody around her will get ready to listen. And I told him what I thought he should hear, the same thing Luis had explained about Mr. Tom being how he was without anyone trying to change him, and us having to decide that it was okay.

"People are just who they are," I said.

CARAMEL

After a couple of months, the swallow babies started hatching. We'd listen to them chirp loudly from their mud nests, knowing that when they grew strong enough, they'd fly south past the equator to Argentina again.

The fog stopped coming in each day, and with the summer came the red tide, uprooted amber seaweed floating in the rolling waves for three weeks straight.

Luis adjusted the ferry schedule for the tourists who'd be arriving, and stocked up on things like Styrofoam coolers and sunscreen.

Pastor Ken practically had an ongoing slide show of his pictures from the annual mission trip to Mexico. I saw it four times. The afternoon he got his haircut I just happened to be in the salon. He told Mama that next spring break I'd be old enough to help out on the trip, and that it would be a good thing to consider. But I saw the strain in Mama's eyes when he mentioned they have no running water for showers or electricity for hair dryers. "It is not the kind of place where one worries about one's appearance," he said, to which Mama looked utterly horrified.

Miss Johnson fixed up our classroom with all our most important projects for the end of the year. Five-paragraph characterization essays. Compare-and-contrast science dioramas. History Day projects. Watercolor paintings. Things people like to see.

I took all of Great-grandmother's stories to Ms. Dixon-Green, our librarian. She said they were a window to my family's history, and helped me bind them into book form so they could be read easier. According to her, Isaac Asimov's *Foundation* should be kept under lock and key, and not thumbed through like an ordinary book. You would've thought I had brought in Isaac Asimov himself by the look on her face when I let her hold that book. But I still keep it next to my bed and read a little of it most nights. I have a feeling my great-grandmother would've wanted it that way, and that she didn't care so much about valuable things being used.

Frankie ran for next year's student council. And won. I could tell the idea of his mama coming back to live near him and Luis settled in because I noticed he didn't tear up her letters anymore.

Instead, he put them in a drawer by the microwave in the back of the Swallow. He hasn't let me see them or anything, but I wouldn't be surprised, because of the way he'd smile when each envelope arrived, if soon he'll be reading them to me aloud. He'll say, "Listen to what my mother wrote today," and things like that.

Sometimes I'd see him reading one of her

letters while sitting on the yellow bench. I'd watch him unfolding the pages, reading them over again and again, like they were filling him up with something.

I imagine one day when his mama hugs him, he'll put his arms around her, too. That these letters she sends are paving the way to family dinners together. That maybe the next time Frankie sees his doctor, the doctor will say, "Frankie, I have good news. You have been miraculously cured of stomachaches."

Marisol won an art award from the city council. It was written up in the newspaper along with a photograph of her. We all said that finally her drawings weren't going to waste on just us. And that soon everyone would know who Marisol Cruz was.

Daddy came back after serving all his time in jail. With longer than normal hair, which Mama would not agree to tend to. She kept insisting there were plenty of other professional stylists in her salon who are almost as talented as she was who could give him a good cut. I think she'd cut his hair if we pushed, but Daddy said not to, that she'd had enough pushing from him.

He got an apartment close to our house. One that I can walk to.

We'd sit on the jetty rocks above the ocean most mornings before I caught the school bus, and have talks about the jobs he was lining up. And how he was going to get all that money back for me. I'd listen to him tell me his plans, and it almost felt like old times again.

"Probation is the time to make things right," he told me. Like each word was the true wish of his heart.

Every day I remember what Luis told me about people being who they are, and that Daddy is trying his best not to gamble. I know this because he goes to meetings each Tuesday, which causes Mama to tear up. She says they are tears of happiness, though, and not to worry any.

I'm just happy to have him back. But I know he means what he says because he's never looked so sure about anything before.

Even Mama agreed after a while that he was trying his best. And one night she let me invite him to have dinner with us.

I cooked everything. Even the dessert. Which was chocolate cake with chocolate frosting, of course.

I have started cooking again. Monday through Friday, I plan the menus for Mama and me. My notebook is stuffed full of recipes from Luis and his Aunt Regina, who has mysteriously taken to sending them in the mail to my house.

The strawberries Luis sells now all have white chocolate swallows drawn on them. I've just about got using the toothpick down. My drawings aren't anything like Marisol's, but people can tell they're birds. They say, "Oh look, chocolate-covered strawberries. And is that a little bird on there? How clever." And then they usually buy one.

My savings account grows a little more each month. Mama says that soon, at the rate I'm going, I'll have enough money to enroll in the first semester of cooking school. Knowing this makes me feel like the luckiest person on Earth, like twirling around the kitchen until I'm dizzy. Imagine being the richest person alive times a million. Well, that's me.

The night Daddy came to dinner, I let Mama help a little with the main course, which was corn-and-beef tamales. But I cooked the white rice for exactly twenty minutes, like it said on the box, and diced the tomatoes and peppers for the salsa.

Mama says that I am a mystery, that my talents are a gift most certainly not from her. Her eyes shine when she says this.

When I set the table after all the cooking was done, I put my plate next to Daddy's. Instead of the usual spot of Mama's plate being next to Daddy's.

Mama said she didn't mind. After all, Daddy and I still had a lot of catching up to do.

I knew he loved me when he brought me a

cookbook, something he'd never done before.

"This is for you, Eleanor," he said, standing in the front door wearing his best shirt.

I glanced at Mama. *He called me Eleanor. Did you hear that?* my eyes said to hers.

"It's even got a recipe for breadfruit in it," Daddy said. "Page seventy-four. See for yourself. There's recipes for those hard-to-cook things in there." He looked at me then like he was seeing me in a new way.

There was not a speck of food left on anyone's plate, and I think it was due to more than just politeness because Daddy said, and I remember his very words, "After eating that dinner, I don't think you need any help from cookbooks. Move over, Betty Crocker," he said.

And it felt better than anything, with his words in my head. And us all sitting at the same dinner table with this feeling floating around like the hour before your birthday party is about to start.

But out of everything that happened, Mama surprised me most of all. Because instead of consulting the planets and stars every morning in the paper, one Sunday she decided to walk to church with me, Luis, and Frankie to listen to Pastor Ken. She stayed for the whole service without rolling her eyes or making a to-do list on the back of the bulletin.

And when we sang songs at the end, Mama stood next to us. I didn't hear her sing, but she did stand up. Like maybe she was thinking about singing as soon as she learned all the words.

So I made sure I said my prayers of thankfulness that night. For Frankie's mama, who'd be coming back soon, and for her sending him those letters that were filling him up inside.

And for Marisol getting her art award and being in the newspaper.

For Mr. Tom getting to his trailer on the island with the supplies Luis gave him.

And for Daddy coming back and trying his hardest to do things differently.

But mostly, I was thankful that I had everything I needed.

So many things happened that Frankie and I started calling it the year the swallows came early. But we both knew it was much more than that.

And when Frankie gave me a See's chocolate at the shop after school one day, I knew things were going to be practically perfect.

Because even though he'd picked that chocolate by pure chance, it just so happened that when I bit into it, I tasted soft *easy*-going caramel, and no coconut flakes.

"It's a good one," I told him, knowing that later I'd add the word *caramel* to the list in my notebook. And that from that day forward, caramel would remind me of things going my way.

"It's nice and smooth," I said.

Frankie just smiled.

ELEANOR ROBINSON'S
(perfected) secret recipe for
chocolate-covered strawberries

INGREDIENTS:

- *10–15 large ripe strawberries with the stems intact (as gigantic as you can find)*
- *8 ounces dark (semisweet) chocolate*
- *4 ounces milk chocolate*
- *¼ cup shortening (Crisco)*

DIRECTIONS:
ask an adult to help

- *Wash and dry strawberries.*
- *In a medium-size saucepan (or a double boiler) on low heat, melt the dark and milk chocolate and shortening. Stir constantly.*

- *Using the stem as a handle, dip each strawberry into the chocolate mixture and twirl it until it is mostly and evenly covered with chocolate. Do not cover the stem part.*
- *Place the berry on a tray lined with waxed paper to dry.*
- *Refrigerate for 30 minutes or more.*
- *Serve.*

P.S. To draw the swallow (like Marisol did), after your strawberries have hardened for 30 minutes in the refrigerator, melt a small amount of white chocolate (½ cup of white chocolate chips works well for this) mixed with a teaspoon of shortening. Dip a toothpick into the mixture while it is still warm, and let the white chocolate drip off onto your strawberry into a pattern. (It is a good idea to practice first on a napkin.) Place strawberries in the refrigerator again until the chocolate is hardened.

ACKNOWLEDGMENTS

I am profoundly grateful for the many people who helped me as I wrote this book over the last three years.

First, there is Jennifer Rofe, the most amazing, incredible agent, who helped me refine my writing beyond what I ever imagined, and asked questions that challenged me to do better.

My SCBWI critique group—Lori Polydoros, Bev Plass, Nancy D'Aleo-Russey, Nadine Fishel, Collyn Justus, and Christian Hill—gave years of kind encouragement and advice.

Louella Nelson, writing professor at University of California at Irvine, listened to early versions of the novel, and pushed me to learn the fundamentals.

Eric Elfman, an unbelievably wise writing coach and adviser, who provided invaluable assistance.

Thomas P. Fitzmaurice, captain of the Redlands Police Department, assisted tremendously with information about California state law.

The staff and volunteers at the Mission San Juan Capistrano in Southern California helped with everything from finding out how many days it takes a swallow egg to hatch, to the exact date and time the swallows arrive back home to the mission each March.

Martha Shimano read many drafts and fixed things like commas and spelling errors (stuff I hate to fix).

Phyllis Westberg, who was my grandmother's literary agent at Harold Ober & Associates, gave almost twenty years of kind encouragement and correspondence. I am truly grateful for her straightforwardness and allowing me to continually ask her opinion.

My mother, Ann Green, who reads *everything*

I write, and then reports back with shining reviews. Her words keep me going through the tough times.

My husband, Brian Fitzmaurice, for everything.

Kathryn Hinds; Molly O'Neill and everyone at the Bowen Press.

And Brenda Bowen, who told me less is more. I could thank you a thousand times, and it wouldn't be enough.